The Secrets of Billie Bright

Susie Day

PUFFIN

PUFFIN

UK | USA | Canada | Ireland | Australia
India | New Zealand | South Africa

Puffin Books is part of the Penguin Random House group of companies
whose addresses can be found at global.penguinrandomhouse.com.

www.penguin.co.uk
www.puffin.co.uk
www.ladybird.co.uk

First published 2016

001

Set in 13/18pt Baskerville MT by Jouve (UK), Milton Keynes
Printed in Great Britain by Clays Ltd, St Ives plc

A CIP catalogue record for this book is available from the British Library

ISBN: 978–0–141–37533–5

All correspondence to:
Puffin
Penguin Random House Children's
80 Strand, London WC2R 0RL

Penguin Random House is committed
to a sustainable future for our business,
our readers and our planet. This book
is made from Forest Stewardship
Council® certified paper.

For Nicky

Hi Mum,

Dad always says 'I wish your mum could see you now' when I put on my new uniform (just to check it all fits, which it obviously doesn't because my shirt is Raffy's old holey one that smells of cupboard and my jumper is Michael's and massive).

But I know you can see me already. I know you're watching over me, because of that time I said 'PLEASE GIVE ME A SIGN' outside the Co-Op and then a pigeon pooed on my Tiny Robot Unicorn Friends backpack.

I actually would've liked a different sort of sign, but I suppose Heaven has a lot of rules.

Anyway, in case you were planning some important sign-sending via poo, I go to Big School today, so that's where you can find me.

I'm not nervous. Even though Mia's going to that weirdo school where they wear stripy blazers and Yasmeen's gone to Devon and I haven't got any best friends any more. And Michael says that the Maths gets well hard. And Raffy says school sucks out your soul one day at a time till you are a Husk Of A Person, and I don't much fancy that.

But Dad made me double-cheese sandwiches. (Dairylea and wiggly mozzarella on crusty white.)

I'll probably actually make new friends in five minutes, because I am, like, fun and interesting and good at making stuff happen, and friends always like that.

I can fetch Michael if anyone tries to flush my head down the bog. (Raffy says that happens too.)

You know I'll be all right. I'm Team Bright and we're The Best.

Tell God I said hi.

Lots of love,
Amen,
Bye

(IN CASE ANYONE NOSY IS LISTENING, I didn't borrow my pants or my bra off my brothers. Mum, I know you knew that already. Heaven doesn't make you stupid, it just makes you far away and a bit quiet.)

The Bright family was quite large for one that was missing a piece.

They lived on Sorrel Street, Kensal Rise, above Dad's café, in a flat that always smelled ever so slightly of sausage rolls.

In charge was Dad, Charlie: big bald head, bigger laugh, made the best cup of tea in all North London. (It said so on the sign in the window.)

Then there were the three Bright brothers:

Gabriel, who had wide-set eyes and was quiet and artistic and always listened, the way big brothers were supposed to, even though he was all grown up now, with a grown-up's life: job, flat in Canary Wharf, shiny shoes.

Next Raffy, who had springy twist-out curls and the sort of stupid little beard you grew when you were seventeen, apparently, and who was not quiet, not at all – never on purpose, always sorry, but in a noisy, messy way that upset things.

Then Michael, who was fourteen and massive, all shoulders and thighs and a beepy alarm on his phone to tell him to do fifty chin-ups.

And last was Billie, who was eleven.

She didn't mind being the only girl, because girls were brilliant. She did mind being the littlest. She'd been trying to catch Michael up for ages. Dad said it didn't work like that; that Michael would keep getting a year older too, just as fast as she did – they all would – but Billie didn't care. She still got to go to Big School now, like him. She wasn't the baby any more. She was Billie Bright, who wore a tie to Kensal Rise Academy and did, like, French and Geometry and Well-Hard Sums.

Or she would be.

Assuming she actually got there.

'I'm ready to go now,' she announced, standing at the top of the stairs with her coat on and her Tiny Robot Unicorn Friends bag packed. 'To school. My new school. For my first day. At my new school.'

Only Raffy was sprawled across the kitchenette

counter, half asleep, and Michael was still in a towel from the shower, squeezing past him to spread crunchy peanut butter on toast.

'Food first,' he said breathlessly. 'Protein window. Coach Jen says I have to replenish my muscles within thirty minutes of exercise.'

Raffy nodded without lifting his head from where it lay, his face half hidden under his hair.

'Yeah, me too,' he mumbled, reaching out to sneak a square of toast.

'Oi! I just ran five k, bruv.'

'And I just scanned maybe a thousand million crates of Moroccan tomatoes for my evil supermarket overlords. I have to replenish my, like, lost integrity.'

Raffy was working night shifts in a warehouse, and came home after 7 a.m., filled with revolutionary zeal and pocketfuls of rejected lettuce that he'd felt sorry for. ('Look at him! He's only a bit wilty!')

Billie looked at the clock and sucked her bottom lip. 'Gabriel wouldn't let me be late,' she said slowly.

Raffy groaned.

'I'll get dressed,' said Michael, mournfully abandoning his toast and running to the bedroom he shared with Raffy.

(The boys were all angels, technically – Gabriel, Raphael, Michael – but Gabriel was the only one who seemed to be taking it seriously. Billie was meant to be an angel too: Ariel, which *was* an angel name, apparently; Mum had waggled a *Children's Illustrated Bible* over her cot to prove it. But Dad had drawn the line at anything so Little-Mermaidy when he went to fill in the form, so Billie she was. It was a relief, to be honest. Not that she planned to turn out evil, exactly. But Raffy said that the responsibility wore you down just a bit.)

Michael reappeared in his uniform, shoelaces trailing. 'Ready?' he said, giving her a wink.

'Ready,' said Billie, winking back. (Hers meant putting a hand over one eye, otherwise it just came out as blinking. She'd get it soon. Dad said you learned loads of new stuff in Year 7.)

Raffy crawled to the sofa and lay on his face, still groaning. 'Don't come back a husk!' he called as they ran down the stairs.

They tried just waving through the steamed-up window of the café as they went past, but Dad wasn't having it.

'Hey! Zahra! Would you look at this girl, uh? You'll never guess who. You'll never guess who this girl is!'

He leaped out from behind the counter, came onto the street, gripped Billie's shoulders and steered her uniformed self inside towards Zahra, who worked in the hair salon next door and saw her roughly every day. Sometimes twice.

'Nooo! That's never Billie!' said Zahra, slapping her hands to her cheeks.

'Same!'

'Nooo!'

'My baby girl's at Big School! And me only twenty-five, eh? Hahaha!'

'Hahaha!'

The café was called The Splendide – no one knew why; it wasn't really – and Raffy had named this version of their father Dad Splendide: the one with the biggest laugh and the biggest smile, trying just that little bit too hard. He wasn't like that at home. Billie wondered if there was a Zahra

Splendide, who went home from over-enthusiastically styling hair and became just Zahra, who got cross about unwashed plates before falling asleep on the sofa.

'Dad?' whispered Billie, looking up. 'We're going to miss the bus.'

'Sorry, angel,' said Dad, switching back to Dad Normale and bending down to look her in the eye. 'You nervous? I could close up – take you in on your first day . . .'

He'd been saying this for a week, even though he'd never, ever closed up, not even when Michael broke his ankle and he spent all night by his hospital bed; up at 5.30 to start all the bread doughs, like clockwork. This morning the red-and-white checked plastic tablecloths were already dotted with empty cups and plates, and there was a queue at the counter. Breakfast was always the busiest time.

For a moment Billie wondered what would happen if she said yes. *Yes please, Dad, I'd like you to take me in on my first day.*

But she knew he would, and then she'd feel awful.

And anyway, she really wasn't nervous. It was exciting, trying new things. Year 6 had got very boring towards the end, surrounded by all these miniature people who still cared about pencil cases and times tables, instead of important eleven-year-old things like exams and the Plight of the Bees. (Billie was quite vexed about the bees.) So she shook her head.

'I'm not nervous, it's exciting, and I will actually always be all right.'

'Go smash it, bright girl,' said Dad, kissing her forehead proudly.

And she dragged Michael out of the café before he could eat a third almond croissant.

Kensal Rise Academy didn't look exciting, to be honest. Half the yard was fenced off with cones and hazard tape, and a building site with scaffolding and rumbling diggers took up a chunk of the playing field. But there was probably excitingness inside. Or round the back, past those bins. There *had* to be – Billie had been looking forward to Big School for ages.

'Wait,' said Michael, hesitating at the gates.

Billie rolled her eyes. 'I keep telling you – I'm not a baby! I'm not nervous! If *you* managed being all new and Year Seven-ish, *I* definitely can.'

'It's different for girls,' said Michael, brow furrowing thoughtfully.

'Not this one. And how would you know anyway? Come on.'

'Wait,' said Michael again. This time he reached down and tugged on her stripy tie till the knot was fat and sloppy. 'Trust me,' he said, with a flash of a smile.

Then he disappeared into a crowd of Year 10 girls, a swingy-ponytailed one slipping her arm through his.

All their ties were fat and sloppy too.

Perfect. Billie beamed as she plunged into the crowd. She was going to be brilliant at this, for definite.

She went to the Lower Hall, where all the Year 7s were waiting to be lined up into classes, and counted the faces of the other black girls, brown girls, hijabi girls, girls she didn't know where to put. Mum had always said people were people – but Billie thought it was easier to think so when all the people on TV looked like you. There were plenty of brown girls, though; more even than at her old school. Lots of all kinds.

But there was hardly anyone she knew from Larkhill Primary. And they were all clustered in groups of their old friends, instead of making themselves available for new ones who might actually be more funny and smart and interesting and would know the rules about ties, actually.

Classes 7A and 7B and 7C and 7D lined up, taking with them Aaliyah (who she'd known since Reception when she used to lick paint off the pot lids in the Art room), and Olivia T (who was the first girl to get a boyfriend, a proper kissing one, which made her briefly famous and special and best – till he dumped her and told everyone it was because she tasted like bacon Wheat Crunchies), and Olivia P (who once drank a spider in a can of Coke on a trip to Thorpe Park) – none of which seemed like good reasons to be new Year 7 best friends anyway.

Billie started to think it was quite selfish of Yasmeen and Mia to have gone to Devon or that weirdo place with the blazers, actually.

Then *Billie Bright* was called to line up in 7E.

The only faces she knew in the 7E line were Bryan, and Big Mohammad, and mean Acacia Morrell, who had fancy new box braids and her eyebrows all painted – while Billie had her big hair in a ponytail, smoothed down with a bit of oil from Zahra, and the eyebrows that came with her face.

Actually Billie thought she might be a bit nervous now, after all, actually.

She looked down the line anxiously, hunting, and then she saw her: a tiny dark-skinned girl in a jumper even more enormous than Billie's, eyes huge, hair half in cornrows, quivering and standing all by herself.

Billie sent the tiny girl her biggest smile.

The tiny girl smiled back shyly.

Yes, Billie thought. *You. You are perfect for best-friending.*

She slid out of the line – but before she could get there, another arm slipped through hers, pinning her back. Another new girl: Chinese-looking, with thick black hair, pink glasses and a pointy chin.

'You look just like my pet rabbit Remington,' she said perkily, patting Billie's hand. 'She gets nervous too. It's perfectly understandable, because it's the first day and tensions are high. Not for me, though. I have a very confident personality and enjoy new challenges – it said so in my last school report. I'm not like a rabbit. I'm more the velociraptor type. Oh, let me just fix your tie – it looks all sloppy! There. Much better. I'm Ruby, by the way. We're going to be best friends.'

2

Billie very much wanted to explain to this poor confused Ruby person that, no, they were not going to be best friends, because Billie was the one who made those sorts of decisions and she'd already chosen that tiny girl. Also her tie didn't need fixing, actually. And she had a confident personality of her own – Zahra from the salon said so. (Well, Zahra said she was 'a gobby little miss', but that meant the same thing, probably.)

But she didn't get to say any of those things. A bell rang, and all the Year 7 class teachers stood at the front of the hall, whispering over clipboards.

There was one young, pretty woman with cat's-eye glasses and a sticky-out dress covered in parakeets, and Billie hoped and hoped for her – but instead 7E got a man teacher, Mr Miller.

Mr Miller did not look as if he understood the excitingness of Year 7. He had a scrubby little grey beard and a grey cardigan with patches on the elbows, and when he spoke, his voice was full of sighs.

'All right, my new minions and underlings, I suppose I can't put it off any longer. Follow me to your certain doom.'

Mr Miller's classroom was upstairs in B Block.

Billie pushed her way in and chose a desk at the front, because that meant you always got asked to hand out the books, and could talk to people on your way round, and accidentally not finish your work but it wasn't your fault because you were doing jobs.

'Oh, well done! I always sit at the front,' said Ruby, sitting in the empty chair beside her.

Then Ruby started putting all her own things out on the desk, as if it was her desk, and she was letting Billie sit there.

So rude.

Mr Miller walked around sighing, slapping down papers in front of them: school contract, homework diary, planner, online portal personal login – each one announced with another deep, weary sigh.

This was a dream, Billie decided. A bad dream,

from which she would wake up, and then go to the proper exciting Big School where people understood how exciting it was supposed to be, instead of being weird and rude and sighing.

Mr Miller stood at the front of the class, yawning at a clipboard. 'Right. Apparently, our esteemed head teacher reckons that if we're going to be lumbered with each other's company, we ought to get to know each other. I want you to tell your neighbour all about yourself. *Three* – it says here – *interesting and surprising facts*. And then you're each going to stand up and introduce your neighbour to the rest of the class. So you'd better listen, hadn't you? You've got five minutes.'

Mr Miller sank into a chair, put his grey shoes up on his desk and closed his eyes.

Billie felt better immediately. She had loads of interesting and surprising facts – and stupid Ruby would realize that, actually, Billie was going to decide if they were best friends, and all the other important decisions. (Yasmeen and Mia had understood this. It actually was completely mean of them, not being here.)

But Ruby started to talk first.

She had a lot more than three interesting and surprising facts:

Her English name was Ruby Stella Goode.

Her Chinese name was Rui Lien, though no one called her that except her mum's family in Taiwan, where they went on holiday once a year.

She lived in Willesden with her mum and stepdad and her new baby sister.

The baby was called Topaz, which is a type of gemstone that's kind of mud-coloured and not as expensive as rubies.

She used to live in Richmond and went to school in Richmond and had been going to go to a new school in Richmond, but then they had moved, which was very sad, but fortunately she had natural charm and would easily make new friends.

She'd chosen her pink glasses when she was nine and her mum wouldn't buy her new ones until she needed a new prescription but they were unrepresentative of her general feelings about the colour pink or her personality in any way, which was actually very sophisticated and gothic.

Her favourite place in the world was Highgate Cemetery. You should probably imagine her wearing thick black eyeliner and long tragic clothes at all times instead of school uniform; she was a very deep, spiritual person with a vivid inner life. She had books about this. She could show you them later.

Billie wanted to say, *Yes, I know all about Highgate Cemetery because my brother Gabriel did a whole art project about it, it's under my bed, and actually I expect I know more about it than you do so I don't need any books* – but Mr Miller stirred from his desk, yawned again, and clapped his hands.

'All right. Now I get to discover how *incredibly* fascinating a roomful of eleven-year-olds can be. When I call your name, stand up and introduce your new "friend".'

One by one, 7E stood up.

Nishat, a girl with a long black plait, had two brothers, a goldfish called Ronaldo, and a deep-seated fear of bees.

Alfie could bend his fingers round the wrong way, and fit his whole fist in his mouth, and once saw Professor X from the *X-Men* films in real life, doing his shopping in Waitrose. (Professor X was buying lemonade and some sort of fish with its head still on.)

The tiny girl Billie had planned to be friends with was called Efe. She was from Nigeria, she lived with her mum and lots of aunties, and she would like to go home please.

Acacia stood up next. 'Uh. This is Sam. She plays football, she once dyed her dog green, and she's a liar.'

'Oi!'

The girl called Sam shot out of her seat and put her face right up close to Acacia's.

Acacia tilted her hip with a hiss. 'She is, though, right? She says she's got two mums and a brother who's also called Sam.'

'Well, I have!'

'She does,' agreed Nishat. 'He's over there.'

A small boy waved a hand apologetically.

'We're twins,' said the girl. 'Duh!'

'Oh,' said Mr Miller, scratching his ear as he looked at his clipboard. 'Sam Paget-Skidelsky. Twice. I thought you were a clerical error.'

'We get that a lot,' said the boy sadly.

The twins didn't look the same, exactly, but they were both freckly, with short floppy brown hair.

Mr Miller coughed and went back to his list. 'Ruby. Tell us about your neighbour.'

Billie sat up straight, ready to explain that *Actually, sir, she can't because she didn't shut up long enough to let me say anything – isn't that rude, sir?* – but instead Ruby turned to face the rest of the class with a smile, smoothing down her navy-blue skirt.

'Class Seven E, allow me to introduce Billie,' she said in a loud, clear voice. 'Billie's very shy and nervous today, so please be kind to her. Her older brother is Michael Bright, in Year Ten. You've probably seen him – he's that big tall gorgeous one—' She broke off to give a little giggle behind her hand. 'Anyway, if you haven't already heard of him, then you will because he's famous, nearly: my stepdad works for NutriGenix – they do all the physio and nutrition for Haringey Rhinos, which is a rugby team – and he says that Michael Bright's going to play for England one day. And . . .' Ruby paused for a dramatic breath, then lowered her voice. 'And Billie hasn't got a mum because her mum is dead. I know, it's so sad, aww.'

'Aww,' chorused 7E awkwardly.

Ruby sat down again, and gave Billie a velociraptor smile. All teeth.

CHAPTER
3

The bus journey home was just as confusing as the rest of the day.

First, the twin Sams followed her all the way back to the flat, on bikes, weaving behind the bus, catching up and staring at her through the misted-up windows.

She had a lot of time to look out of the bus window because of the second thing, which was the swingy-ponytailed girl – who sat in Billie's seat next to Michael all the way home, kissing his lips over and over again, and taking pictures of herself doing it on her phone.

'Sorry,' he mumbled, looking sheepish when they jumped off the bus, leaving the girl drawing steam hearts on the window inside. 'That's Natasha. She's. Um. A friend.'

'She was friendly,' said Billie, watching curiously as the two Sams sped off up Sorrel Street, the girl one staring back over her shoulder. 'Are you really going to play rugby for England one day? Like, *really* – like rugby on the telly and in the news?'

Michael looked shifty. 'Um. Well, maybe. There's England under-sixteen tryouts soon, and if I made the squad, I'd get more coaching, and then maybe . . . Who told you?'

Billie explained.

'Oh yeah? Pete – I know him – he gives us massages and sports drinks and that. I might not be good enough, though. They might not want me. Probably not.'

Billie poked him crossly in his gigantic shoulder. 'You're Team Bright, stupid. Course you'll be good enough.'

Michael dipped his head. 'Maybe. Just . . . don't tell anyone, yeah? Our secret?'

He meant Dad. Dad, who would make him training timetables and put motivational quotes in Michael's lunch box. Dad, who would worry.

'Our secret,' she said, hooking thumbs with him to lock it up safe.

Michael smiled, wide and warm.

It was happening already: grown-upness. Annoying baby sisters couldn't keep secrets. Proper old going-to-Big-School sisters could be trusted.

Then Michael slotted his key into the lock of their peely-paint blue front door, smushed her into the wall and raced up the stairs ahead of her to snag the good armchair, cackling triumphantly all the way.

Well. It wasn't like she expected it to happen all at once.

She left him flipping through music channels and went up to her little attic bedroom at the very top of the flat: small, with a sloping ceiling, and all hers (apart from the Transformers wallpaper and all the boys' old things in her cupboards and under her bed, from when it was Gabriel and Raffy's).

Usually she'd put on a Disney soundtrack (*The Lion King* or *Lilo & Stitch* were her current favourites) and curl up on her bed to play *Bubble Gems* on her phone, using her stuffed Zanzibar Tiny Robot Unicorn Friend as a pillow. But she hesitated as she pulled off her tie and hung it up. Disney songs and stuffed unicorns might not be entirely grown up and Big-School-like. Ruby probably listened to posh violin music at her house. Or industrial goth shouting.

Then she remembered that Ruby was stupid and awful and also not here, so she put on 'Circle of Life' at volume eleven and sang along.

It was Raffy's turn to cook tea that night so she knew it would be beans, or burned, or both, before the smoke alarm even went off.

'It's not my fault!' he yelped, flapping around the kitchenette in pyjama bottoms as an ominous smog billowed out from under the grill.

'Ah, what every customer loves to hear,' called Dad, thumping up the stairs.

The Splendide closed at 6.30 p.m. on the dot Monday to Saturday, and Dad liked a mug of tea and a plate of food ready and waiting by 6.33 precisely – except once a week, when he knocked off early and he and Billie cooked it together.

'Come on then, angel. How did it go?' said Dad, carefully lowering himself into the sofa beside her with his mug of tea.

Their sofa was moss-green and elderly; the kind that drooped in the middle, so if more than one of you sat down, you ended up comfily rolled together. Dad said it was the sign of a happy home if even the furniture was well-loved. And it meant that no one ever got shouted at if they spilled fizzy Vimto all down the cushions. For example.

'Yeah, Bills – you a husk yet?' asked Raffy, rattling plates out of the cupboard.

'Did anyone flush you?' asked Michael.

'Or lock you in a locker?' asked Raffy.

'Or zip you into a sports bag?'

'Or tip you into a bin?'

Dad threw a hand up. 'What? Where am I sending you kids?'

'Oh, that's nothing – they go easy on Year Sevens,' said Michael helpfully.

Dad took a big anxious gulp of tea.

'They're just winding you up,' said Billie, patting his arm comfortingly and shooting the boys a look.

It was best not to talk about bad things when Dad hadn't had his tea. Or ever. So she decided to skip the part where everyone in 7E had wanted to know *all* about her dead mum – and it turned out that 'cancer' and 'when I was five' weren't interesting enough answers – and how she'd actually eaten her double-cheese sandwiches by herself, in the spidery toilets by C Block.

'It was fine, Dad,' she promised, tucking her head under his arm and resting her chin on his chest. 'I liked it. I've got nice teachers, apart from Mr Miller, who is all grey and sad, like Eeyore. I'm going to join band and art club and environmental club, and basically all the clubs. And I'm in Wimbledon house, which is green, so everyone says it's like Slytherin, but Mrs Shah – she's our Head of House – she says it just means we're the house everyone's scared of because we're going to win. I don't know what we're going to win, but I want to.'

Raffy groaned as he hunted for cutlery. 'Nooo, it's started already. Your conversion into a drone. They just want to teach you how to be a worker bee, Bills. Just a bee. Never a butterfly.'

'You do know that bees don't grow into butterflies, son?' asked Dad, looking wary.

'I've read *The Very Hungry Caterpillar*, Dad. I'm good.'

Michael got a faraway look on his face. 'A slice of salami,' he murmured.

Raffy brought the plates over: fish fingers, beans, potato waffles – each waffle with a single wedge of orange placed on top.

'It's like a garnish,' he explained proudly.

'It is *like* a garnish,' agreed Dad. 'Thank you, Raff. Say grace, Bills?'

'For our slices of orange which rolled on the warehouse floor, Lord, we are truly thankful,' she said. She smiled up at the photo of Mum in the alcove behind the TV too, just to make it extra religious.

'Amen,' said Dad.

Michael ate his with ketchup.

He didn't ask for seconds.

The next day Billie knotted her tie fat and sloppy again.

Ruby's fingertips wriggled when she saw it. Billie watched her eyes darting, noting the knots on other people's ties, and later, when she came back from the toilets after morning break, Ruby's tie was suddenly fat and sloppy too.

It was exactly what Yasmeen and Mia would've done. Perhaps it was going to be OK being friends with Ruby, after all.

That morning Billie had her first English class – with the pretty parakeet-skirt teacher. Her name was Miss Eagle, and she was even prettier up close: chestnut hair pinned up on top of her head, and bright red lips. This time she was wearing a spotty red dress that stuck out and brushed against the tables, a black cardigan with red buttons, and shiny black T-bar shoes with little white ankle socks.

'You look like a ladybird, miss,' said Big Mohammad.

'Thank you, Mohammad,' said Miss Eagle.

Billie wasn't sure it was a compliment, but now it felt like one.

She decided that Miss Eagle was probably quite clever.

Miss Eagle made them all do a short writing test: *Write a letter to an alien, telling them what it means to be in Year 7.* Billie's letter politely suggested that the alien found someone better qualified, what with it being only her second day and spending quite a lot of the first one in a spidery toilet. Ruby (who was in the seat next to her again – they'd both run for the front desk) meanwhile wrote three pages and drew a map of the school, which was just showing off and not even English anyway.

Then Miss Eagle sat on the edge of her desk, swinging her shiny shoes.

'Now, I have the *most* exciting announcement, Seven E!' she said. 'You may have noticed all the building work on the playing field . . . Well, as some of you will have heard, that building site is going to be a new sports complex! Not just for the school but for the whole community. By December we'll have an all-weather floodlit football pitch, a fitness suite, and an indoor sports hall for basketball, badminton, dance classes – you name it. The hall will also be used for the school's theatre productions and musical performances, so if you're not sporty there's still plenty for you to look forward to.'

7E was impressed. 7E made murmuring noises about not minding the field being all mud and diggers if they were going to have a floodlit football pitch and a massive sports hall.

'Will we really get to use it, miss?' asked Sam, putting her hand up. 'Will we have to pay?'

'Yes, you will use it, and no, you won't have to pay – not during school hours, anyway.'

'Can we do roller-skating in it, miss?'

'Hmm. I don't know. I don't see why not.'

'Will there be a café, miss?'

'Maybe.'

'I don't intend to be impolite, miss, but what does a sports complex have to do with English?'

That was Edmond Hudson, who made Billie

think of skimmed milk: delicate white skin and pale blond curls.

Miss Eagle smiled. 'Excellent question, Edmond. Since the complex is being built on school property, the head thought it was important for you all to be closely involved. So the school is asking students to come up with the right name for the facility. As you'll have noticed, many important buildings are named after famous or important people; people who've made a difference to the world.'

'Like Ronald McDonald's Play Factory, miss?'

'Not quite, Mohammad.'

''S all right, miss, I was only joking.'

'Good to know. What I was thinking of was something a bit more personal. Now, brainstorm, please!'

She switched on the whiteboard.

WHAT IS A HERO?

7E called out suggestions, and she typed in whatever was said.

Someone with superpowers

Batman, who doesn't have superpowers but is still
a superhero

Someone who saves the world

Someone who keeps trying, even when it's tough

Malala Yousafzai

Harry Potter

And Hermione

Rama

Thor

Frodo

Jacqueline Wilson

Ian Wright

Gandhi

Florence Nightingale

Nishat's uncle

Billie thought it was a pretty weird list – but
Miss Eagle seemed happy.

'And why are these people heroes?'

'Because Thor's got a massive hammer, miss.'

'True – but none of the others do.'

'Because they're famous?'

'Hmm. Nishat's uncle's not famous – so far as

I know. No? And some of these are fictional. Harry Potter's famous in the books, but Hermione isn't. Frodo isn't. What makes all these heroes?'

'Us,' said Billie, putting her hand up. 'We like them. We want to be them.'

Miss Eagle's red-lipsticky lips turned up in a smile.

Billie felt Ruby's pointy chin turn her way, and she shuffled smugly in her seat.

'I don't want to be Frodo – he has to fight loads of Orcs and stuff so he can throw a stupid magic ring into a volcano instead of staying at home and eating loads,' said Sam. 'And Malala got shot in the head.'

'She's still amazing, though,' said Nishat.

'Maybe not *be* them, then. But . . .'

'We want to be like them,' said the boy Sam, very quietly.

'They're role models,' said Ruby.

'Exactly!' Miss Eagle smiled again, as if she'd been waiting for someone to say that, and Ruby shuffled smugly in her seat right back, even though she hadn't even put up her hand or anything.

Miss Eagle flashed up a new screen.

WHO IS YOUR HERO?

'I want you to think about the people you admire and respect; figures you look up to. Your role models. And I want you to take your time, because here's the really exciting thing: whoever you choose could be the name lighting up the new sports hall.'

She tapped a key, and the whiteboard changed again: a 3D drawing of a squarish tan-brick building with huge blue capitals across the front wall above the entrance:

MISS EAGLE SPORTS &
LEISURE COMPLEX

'Just a little artist's impression to get you thinking!' she said, her cheeks pinking. 'This is your personal project for this term: to select and research the hero or role model of your choice; to give an oral presentation and produce a written project – using persuasive language – explaining why they deserve to have their name up there.'

Miss Eagle really *was* clever, thought Billie, because actually that was just school and homework.

But once Miss Eagle had told Madison she could do her project on Spider-Man if she wanted, 7E decided that it was fun again.

'I'm not saying that the Spider-Man Sports and Leisure Complex is very likely to win,' she added. 'Mrs Cooper will have the final decision. But if you do a good project, who knows? Either way, very soon there will be a real name on a real sign on a real building, and one of you in Year Seven will have chosen it. So – choose wisely.'

Billie pressed her lips together in a secret smile. She knew *exactly* who she was going to pick.

CHAPTER
5

Going home on the bus was a lot like yesterday –
with the twin Sams mysteriously tailing her home
as before, and swingy-ponytailed Natasha kissing
Michael all over his face: cheeks, ears, eyebrows,
neck. She couldn't be very good at kissing, poor
thing, Billie thought sadly. Everyone knew it was
meant to be on the lips.

But at the same time, it wasn't like yesterday
at all.

She glowed from the inside every time she
thought about the Hero project, like a little flame
had been lit under her ribs. It burned brightly as
she hurried upstairs, and hung up her tie, and
hummed the theme from *Brave* over her homework. She kept noticing she was grinning, and
remembering again, and feeling it light her up.

It was still there at tea time, when Dad's trainers
wearily thudded up the stairs.

'All right, bright girl? How did it go? Still like it?' he asked, sinking into the sofa beside her, mug raised up carefully as they rolled together like ships at sea.

This time it was easy to beam back. 'It was brilliant.'

'Aw, yeah, Dad, guess what,' said Michael, carrying over plates heaped up with chicken, broccoli and rice. (When Michael cooked, there was always a lot.) 'They're building this new sports complex thing – like, a big hall, and a football pitch—'

'That's what I was going to say!' protested Billie as Raffy stumbled out of the bedroom, hair jammed into a hat, still in pyjama bottoms.

'Could you be going to say it a bit quieter?' he mumbled, rubbing his face sleepily as Michael handed him a plate too.

'It's just, like, a building site at the moment,' Michael continued. 'But it's going to have an outdoor track, a gym, a weights room. Mr Baroni says he's going to make sure I get to go first thing, extra hours – and after school.'

Dad smiled. 'That's great, Michael. You keep

aiming high, yeah? Never give anyone any reason to say no.'

Michael nodded, and threw Billie a secret wink.

Raffy poked gloomily at his chicken.

'Wait – he's missed out the most important bit!' said Billie. 'Year Seven get to name it. We all have to pick a hero and write a project about our hero, and then one of them will be the name. Of the whole place. Like, the Spider-Man Sports and Leisure Complex. Only Miss Eagle says it probably won't be that.'

'I wouldn't think so, no,' said Dad slowly.

''S not fair,' said Michael through a mouthful of rice. 'How come it's just Year Sevens who get to pick a name?'

'Because Year Tens would come up with stupid names with swears in, bruv, because fourteen-year-old boys are disgusting,' grunted Raffy.

Michael looked forlorn. 'Not all of us.'

'That's still not the most important bit!' said Billie, thumping the sofa with the bottom of her knife and fork. 'The important bit is, *I'm* going to win the competition. To name the sports complex. With my Hero project.'

'Ambitious. I like it,' said Dad. 'Who's it going to be?'

Billie rolled her eyes. Then she looked up at the alcove behind the TV, feeling that warm glow inside burning brighter than ever. 'Duh. Who do you think? Mum. She's my hero. And I'm going to win, and her name will be on the sports hall at school for ever and ever.'

Dad's fork stopped halfway to his mouth.

Everything went quiet.

'That's nice, Bills,' said Michael slowly. 'She'd like that. Right, Dad?'

Dad put down his fork and did a little cough. 'Yeah, angel. That's . . . You just took me by surprise is all. It's sweet. A sweet idea. Isn't it, Raff?'

But Raffy had a strange, hurt look on his face.

'Isn't it, Raff?' said Billie, confused.

'Uh-huh,' he mumbled, to the carpet.

But he didn't eat any more of his chicken and rice and broccoli.

And after everything was washed up and put away, he crashed about in the bedroom, then went out, hours before his shift, his big boots going *thump-thump-thump* as he jumped down the stairs, with a bang from the front door.

Hi Mum,

This is probably a stupid question, but do you watch over all of us? Dad and Gabriel and Raffy and Michael and Uncle Fed and everyone, as well as me?

It would be a bit rude if you didn't. Just saying.

Anyway, if you could do an extra watch over Raffy, that would be good. Dad said it wasn't my fault, he still gets sad sometimes about you, and not to worry. But Michael got to eat his chicken anyway so it wasn't all bad.

Could you watch over Michael too to help him with his training? I know he will be trying out for England U16s, not Wales U16s – but I bet you'd cheer him on anyway. Raffy says national boundaries are just invisible fences we build to hurt each other. Or something like that. Anyway, you're half Italian and half Welsh so Michael's only a quarter leek-flavoured.

You don't need to watch over me because I'm already brilliant. (Though if you felt like sending some poo to drop on Ruby's head, that would be fine.)

Anyway, obviously you're my hero. You were

41

very brave about having cancer and dying – everyone said so.

Not exactly like Thor or Harry Potter. Not like Malala Yousafzai.

And you didn't win.

But you're still the person I most want to be like.

You, and Elsa from *Frozen*, and Miss Eagle. I like her lots. She's what Dad calls 'a well-put-together woman'. (Don't worry, you are still the password for his computer.) I'm planning to be a well-put-together woman, once I've grown a bit taller and rounder and bought some new shoes. Unless that isn't what it means. Do you put yourself together, or does God do it when you're a baby? Am I well put together already?

I have got boobies. But small ones. I reckon this leaves less room in there for cancer so I hope they don't suddenly go all, like, bazonga on me.

Whatever I am, I'm glad you're here to watch me being it.

I hope you like my project idea. I think the CARIAD BRIGHT SPORTS & LEISURE COMPLEX would inspire loads of people, much more than a Spider-Man one. And even if I don't win, I get to spend all term thinking about you, even more than usual.

Lots of love,
Amen,
Bye

CHAPTER
6

By the next morning Raffy had cheered right up. (His mate Abdelrahman had let him have a go on a forklift, and he managed to knock over sixty-four crates of bananas. Billie wasn't sure if it was on purpose or not – but he seemed happy.)

Michael was happy too, in between having his chin kissed while staring lovingly at the building site. It turned out that Ruby was right: he *was* sort of famous. Just that morning three people had asked Billie if she was Michael Bright's little sister. And whenever she saw him in the corridors or the yard (he was easy to spot, a head taller than all his friends), there was always a comet trail of people following behind him.

This was the annoying thing about Big School, then. You had to start at the bottom. If Miss Eagle had asked Billie to write a letter to an alien about being a Year 7 today, she would've put:

Dear Space Alien,

   Bring a small backpack because the bigger
kids squish you against walls in the corridor
between classes otherwise. Also, don't have RE
then Science on your timetable because they
are a hundred miles apart and Ms Wright-
Chesterton will threaten to set your books on
fire with a Bunsen burner for arriving late
(TRUE). On Wednesday's hot lunch is curly
fries so everything smells like curly fries.

Kind regards,
Billie Bright, 7E
P.S. No one writes letters now. Get Snapchat, Space
Alien.

'I couldn't find you in the dining hall yesterday, or
the day before,' said Ruby when the lunch bell rang
at the end of Maths. 'I thought maybe you'd got
lost. It is *very* confusing, starting at a big new school.'
She slipped her arm through Billie's. 'You can sit
with me so you don't look lonely and pathetic.'

   'I eat mine at the picnic tables,' said Billie firmly,
reclaiming her arm. 'No one cool eats packed lunch
in with hot lunch.'

'Yeah, I heard that,' said the girl Sam, following them down the stairs.

Tiny Efe nodded nervously too.

Billie raised an eyebrow, waiting. Ruby's mouth pressed into a cross wiggly line – but she let Billie lead the way.

(*Yes*, thought Billie. *And ner, and I win, and I hope no one tells you about me eating my lunch in the spidery toilets ever.*)

The picnic tables were hard plastic, sculpted to look like real wood, lined up behind the PE changing rooms at the edge of the field. It was a bit close to the building site; they could hear the grinding whirr of a cement mixer, and the builders singing along to the radio. But there were lots of Year 8s and 9s out there, and no other Year 7s.

The four of them huddled in their coats and unpacked their lunches.

'Now, I've been thinking, and I've worked out a plan,' said Ruby, unwrapping a slice of leftover pepperoni pizza.

'About what?' said Sam, who had a hummus sandwich and carrot sticks, and kept eyeing the pizza.

(Billie had double-cheese again, this time on

poppy-seed bread, with cherry tomatoes in a pot, which was basically pizza, nearly. Better, actually, because it was fresh, not left over.)

'The Hero project, of course,' said Ruby. 'We need to win, instead of someone boring and stupid, or our school will have a stupid sports complex name and we'll be losers. We should do a survey, to find out what everyone else is choosing. Then once we know what's the least-stupid most popular choice, all of us choose that too.'

'What if I want to choose my own hero?' asked Sam, sounding doubtful.

'You won't win,' said Ruby. 'Loads of people will choose the same hero, you know they will. Because most people are stupid. And if half of Year Seven all choose the same hero, Mrs Cooper will *have* to pick one of them.'

'What if most people choose Spider-Man?' asked Efe, in a small voice, munching her way through a huge ice-cream tub of spicy rice. 'I don't like spiders. Or Spider-Men.'

'It won't be Spider-Man,' said Ruby confidently. 'It wouldn't be allowed; it would be, like, fake advertising. Or copyright. Or something.'

47

'She won't just pick the most popular one, though, will she?' said Sam. 'She'll pick someone all inspirational and mushy who ran a marathon even though they were really old. Or someone local and famous and dead.'

Billie coughed, and put down her sandwich. 'Actually . . . Ruby, I like your idea, it's really clever – but actually I've chosen my hero already, and I don't want to change it.'

Ruby's mouth went into an even crosser, wigglier line when Billie told them who she'd chosen.

'That's really nice,' said Efe. 'I hope you win.'

'Yeah,' said Sam. 'I mean, if none of us do.'

'Thanks,' said Billie. 'And I'll still help with the survey, Ruby.'

Ruby's cross mouth twisted up into a smile, and she tilted her head on one side and patted Billie's hand. 'Aw, thanks. You are *so* sweet. But it's OK, the three of us can do it without you.'

Ruby supplied them all – except Billie – with a clipboard, two pencils (in case of snapping) and a printed survey with six questions, and they spent the rest of the lunch hour going round the dining hall with clipboards to 'gather the relevant data'.

Billie ate her double-cheese sandwiches by herself, reading a book about owls and definitely not minding.

'There were a lot of Spider-Men,' confided Efe when they came back, looking distressed. 'Really very many.'

'And everyone kept asking *why* we wanted to know,' said Sam.

'For *science*,' said Ruby firmly, gathering up the last surveys. 'To be scientific. Sam, your handwriting is awful – this looks like it says Nusrat's hero is Black Window.'

'Maybe it is,' said Sam.

Ruby took all the pages home, and the next day she produced a neatly printed set of pie charts and bar graphs showing the distribution of votes, bound in a pink plastic folder.

'My mum's a biochemist when she isn't looking after the baby,' she said. 'She says you can't decide anything important without data.'

'What's that?' asked Efe, pointing at an orange splodge on the folder.

Ruby paled, and emptied the pages out – but there were little carroty splodges like fingerprints on those too, and the back page was quite scrumpled up.

'Never mind,' she snapped, smoothing out the crumpled page. 'Here, look. Spider-Man did get lots of votes – but I've discounted him. And I've ignored all the outliers – those are statistical anomalies that aren't relevant to the data set, because they only got one vote. Like Judi Dench, and Captain Samazing.'

'And Billie's mum,' said Efe.

'Exactly,' said Ruby.

Billie felt an unhappy fluttering in her insides. She didn't like Mum being a statistical anomaly.

'So, if you look at page seven, you'll see it's a tie between Mo Farah, Ian Wright and Jessica Ennis-Hill.'

'Who's Ian Wright?' asked Efe.

'Footballer,' said Sam. 'Lives in one of those massive houses by the park – so maybe if he wins, he'll come and open it. Cut a ribbon with a big pair of scissors and let you take a selfie. I don't think Malala's going to do that. I still don't want to pick him, though. I think it should be Mo or Jess.'

Ruby nodded. 'And we should pick a girl to win, because, erm, sisterhood and things. So – we should all do our projects on Jessica Ennis-Hill, and then we'll win. You can come to my house after school and we can work on it together, all the way till Christmas. Oh, apart from you, Billie. You can work on yours by yourself. Agreed?'

Hi Mum,

I think the JESSICA ENNIS-HILL SPORTS & LEISURE COMPLEX is going to win more than the CARIAD BRIGHT SPORTS & LEISURE COMPLEX, because Jessica Ennis-Hill is in adverts for being sporty, whereas I think I remember you being on the sofa eating a whole mint Viennetta while watching *Strictly*. Sorry about it, but maybe you should've been a bit more athletic if you wanted to have a sports complex named after you later.

I'm still doing you for my Hero project, though. It's going to be brilliant. It might even be so brilliant it wins anyway, and then Ruby will feel really stupid for making pie charts for no reason.

Ruby is definitely a lot less like Yasmeen and Mia than I would like, and if she went away, then me and Sam and Efe could be three friends, which is the best number of friends. But I think Ruby knows that too.

Year 7 is actually quite hard, actually.

But I'm still smashing it and being my best, because that's what Team Bright do.

Maybe I should go out running with Michael in the mornings. I could be sporty. What do you think?

Really, a sign would be good.

Lots of love,
Amen,
Bye

CHAPTER
7

On Saturday morning Raffy came home with drooping shoulders and no wilty lettuces, bruised oranges or anything else in his pockets.

'You're back late,' said Billie, who was curled up in pyjamas with buttered toast and *Toy Story 3*.

'Bruv, don't tell me,' said Michael, pausing in his sit-ups.

'It's not my fault!' Raffy sank into the sofa and hugged a cushion as Billie rolled inevitably towards him. 'They've got this whole system thing where they get fresh stuff that comes in – like fruit and veg and that – and then it gets rejected for being a bit ugly. It's fine, you could eat it – it's just kind of knobbly-looking. Like, you're being judgemental about vegetables now, man? This carrot does not conform to your unrealistic beauty standards? These potatoes are, like, in need of Photoshop?'

'What did you do?' asked Michael, looking

worried. Billie wasn't sure if it was more for Raffy or the potatoes.

'They just throw all that stuff away! It goes in a big bin and they take it to be, like, mushed back into the ground or whatever! When there's child poverty and homelessness and that!'

'So . . .' said Billie.

'I kind of, um, liberated the stuff on its way to the reject bin, and put it in the back of Abdelrahman's van.'

'You stole it?' said Michael, sitting up with a jerk.

'They were throwing it away! You can't steal stuff if it's already been thrown out!' Raffy squished the cushion harder. 'Only . . . they said it was still their property, so it turns out you can.'

'Fired?' asked Billie gently.

Raffy nodded.

She offered him her toast, and rested her head on his shoulder while he ate it.

Raffy got fired a lot. It was never for anything really *awful*; just little things, like forgetting that if you worked in a restaurant, they didn't like it when you wore flip-flops and shorts, the same ones, three days in a row. Or delivering pizza on a moped, and eating some of the pizza before you delivered it. Or being an elf in a Christmas market, holding a sign saying FESTIVE BARGAINS! with an arrow pointing the wrong way for five hours before anyone noticed.

Sometimes it was for horrible reasons too, like his hair. Raffy was light – lighter than all of them – and if he cut it short, he got called white boy, so he liked it in locs, or cornrows, or a twist-out into big springy corkscrews like now. Once he'd been fired from a cheese factory because there wasn't a hairnet big enough to fit it all in, which Gabriel said was illegal and he could sue them, but Raffy said it smelled funky in there anyway and not to bother. He always picked up another job in a day or two anyway.

'Do you want me to tell Dad?' asked Billie, peering up.

Dad never shouted when Raffy lost a job. But he got that crinkle – the one in the middle of his eyebrows – and looked tired – even more than usual – and they heard him shuffling about late at night, making cocoa when he couldn't sleep.

Raffy shook his head. 'Nah. I'll do it. It'll be

OK, though. Abdelrahman's mate Dev works for a taxi place, says he might give me a job.'

'Does Dev know you can't drive?' asked Billie.

'Ye-ah,' said Raffy, not very convincingly. 'It'll be fine. I'm just bummed about those potatoes, bruv.'

'Yeah,' sighed Michael, starting his sit-ups again. 'Imagine all them chips.'

Michael went off to rugby training.

Raffy went to bed.

Billie washed up, put on two loads of laundry while watching *Mulan*, and at lunch time she went to The Splendide for a bacon bap.

'Your usual, madame?' said Gloria.

Gloria worked there on Saturdays, and most mornings. She was nice to Billie; too nice sometimes – all bosomy hugs without asking if you wanted one. But she made really good bacon baps, better than Dad even – crispy, with a lightly toasted roll and loads of sauce.

Billie sat in her usual Saturday chair at the draughty table no one liked, and took three big bites of bap before she realized she was being stared at.

It was the twin Sams from school, and two women Billie decided must be their mums: one cardiganish and comfortable-looking with wispy hair tucked into a bun; one with short purplish hair, oblong glasses and a MS MARVEL T-shirt. They were all sitting at the next-door table, eating baguettes, dropping crumbs on a little brownish-grey dog tucked under the boy's feet.

'I told you!' said Sam, glaring at the two women. Then she looked back at Billie. 'I said you lived here, and they all said, *No one lives in a café*, and I said, *She does, though*, and they said, *What, that dodgy-looking greasy spoon by the bus stop?* and I said, *Yeah*, and they still didn't believe me, so I said we should come and then they'd be proved wrong, and they have been, so ner, she so totally does actually live in a café.'

The boy Sam frowned thoughtfully at Billie, then peered under the red-and-white checked tablecloths as if looking for beds.

'I don't think that was *quite* how it went,' said the purple-haired mum.

The other mum turned round in her chair to smile at Billie. 'Hello. Nice to meet you. Have you just started Year Seven too?'

Billie had to answer all the usual questions about uniforms and teachers, while eating the rest of her bacon bap, and being watched by four people and a dog.

(Billie was not fond of dogs. They were licky and bitey, and you couldn't tell what they were thinking.)

Dad came over and was Dad Splendide at them, in a rescuing sort of way. 'Coffees, ladies? We do proper coffee here, any way you like. Desserts too – apple pie, chocolate brownie? All homemade, on the premises.'

But the purple-haired mum said she'd baked a courgette cake just that morning, thank you, and just the bill would do nicely.

Sam coughed loudly. Then the cardiganish mum jumped in her chair, as if she'd been kicked sharply on the shin.

'Perhaps Billie might like to come back to ours – to help us eat that cake?' she said.

Sam nodded vigorously. 'Please say yes. Otherwise I'll have to have it in my lunch box, and it's disgusting.'

CHAPTER

8

The Paget-Skidelskys lived at the other end of
Sorrel Street, the posh end; quiet and leafy, away
from the shops and bins and bus stops, and Bad
Kev who weed in the doorways. Instead of a flat
they lived in half a big chilly brick house, with a
front garden and a red-brick pillar at the end of
the path with a gold plaque on it: DR G. PAGET &
DR K. SKIDELSKY: FAMILY THERAPY AND CHILD
PSYCHOLOGY. Dr Paget (she was the comfy
cardiganish one) gave therapy sessions to sad
families on the plush golden sofas of their front
room. Dr Skidelsky (the purple-haired one who
kept shouting at the dog, which was called Surprise
and kept chewing her trainer) taught university
students, and did research.

Both of them were very interested in Billie's
three older brothers, and just a dad.

'Don't tell them anything!' warned Sam as

they all sat down round a big white kitchen table. 'They'll ask sneaky nosy questions, and next thing you know she'll have written a book about you.'

The boy Sam nodded wanly.

Billie thought having a book written about you sounded pretty sweet, actually; if it was a good one, like *How to Train Your Dragon*.

But apparently Dr Skidelsky wrote the sort of books that had footnotes and long words in, not dragons.

'And we're not being sneaky or nosy,' said Dr Paget, smiling as Dr Skidelsky produced the disgusting courgette cake and handed out slices. 'We're just interested. What's that like, Billie, being the only girl in a house full of boys?'

'Mum *Gen*,' muttered the boy Sam, looking mortified.

'Don't,' hissed Sam. 'It's like you're pointing out who isn't there.' Her eyes darted between them, as if she was worried one of them might vanish too. As if not having a mum was catching.

Dr Paget watched Billie carefully, then smiled. 'I think Billie knows who isn't there, hmm? Do you mind me asking about your family, Billie?'

Billie thought about it as she sniffed her slice of cake. It looked normal enough, apart from being faintly green, but Sam was busily feeding hers to the dog under the table. 'No,' she said eventually. 'So long as you don't think I have to do all the cooking or cleaning just because I'm the girl.'

Dr Skidelsky grinned. 'Oh, we're definitely not going to think that.'

'Then . . . I like it. They look after me. Gabriel used to pick us up from school sometimes and take us for ice creams. Raffy watches Disney films with me 'cos he likes the songs. Michael is good for walking between me and dogs on the pavement because he knows I don't like dogs. Sorry – I'm sure yours is a nice one – I just don't. We're a Team, Dad says. I like that.'

She paused and tried a small nibble of cake. It wasn't disgusting at all; just a bit odd-smelling.

'They do leave hairy chin bits and foam and mud in the bathroom, though. And Michael and Raffy have to keep their stinky trainers in a special box that if you open it without holding your breath you might actually be sick. You can't save one last square of chocolate or pudding for later when you're hungry again because when you come back, they'll have eaten it, even though it was obviously yours and you were saving it, obviously. And . . . sometimes they're just a bit *big*, you know? They take up lots of space. But that's OK. I can take up lots of space too.'

Billie stopped talking, feeling her cheeks go warm.

'See?' said Sam. 'Sneaky *and* nosy. Can we go now?'

'Go on,' said Dr Paget, with a soft smile. 'And thank you, Billie. I found that very interesting.'

Sam groaned, grabbed Billie's elbow and hauled her up the green-carpeted stairs, Surprise bouncing alarmingly close at her heels.

Sam's bedroom was smallish and cosy, with a metal-framed bed, a furry blue rug, and walls that were almost completely covered with football posters. There were a few of the England Lionesses, but most were of big green stadiums with Brazilian flags, and a brown girl with a long dark ponytail and sparkly brown eyes, caught mid-kick, or being lifted in the air by her team-mates.

'Do you know who that is?' asked Sam hopefully.

Billie had to shake her head. 'Sorry.'

Sam moaned, and flopped onto her bed, Surprise jumping up after her and lying on her belly. 'No one does. I tried paying people with KitKat Chunkys to put her top on Ruby's stupid hero survey, but then I ran out of KitKat Chunkys, and even the ones who got one put stupid Ian Wright instead.'

'Who is she?'

Sam sat up eagerly. 'This is Marta. She's the best footballer in the whole world; not just women's – everyone, everywhere. She won Player of the Year five times in a row. She's scored more goals in the World Cup than anyone, ever.' She rolled over and pointed at the posters on the wall in turn. 'This is her playing for FC Rosengård. This is her playing for Brazil – that was the goal that got her the Golden Boot. And . . . these are me.'

Sam pointed to a row of glossy team photos of small girls in yellow T-shirts and shiny shorts, and clippings from the local paper.

'Kensal Rise Kites – I'm their best striker. Because of Marta. She's why I wanted to learn how to play, ever since I was little. I wanted to be just like her. I still want to be just like her. She's . . . just amazing. At the Player of the Year ceremony they made her wear high heels and a little dress, but you could tell she wanted to be back out there on the pitch in her kit, doing her thing.' Sam scooped Surprise up into her arms. 'She makes me feel like it's OK to be me,' she said in a softer voice. 'If it wasn't for Marta, I would never have thought I could play. I wouldn't even have tried.'

Sam lay back down on the bed and let Surprise lick her on the nose.

Billie sat down too and stroked the dog, just once, to try. It didn't bite. But she didn't think she wanted to stroke it again.

'You want to do Marta for your Hero project, don't you?'

Sam nodded gloomily. 'There's no point, though. She's not going to win if people wouldn't even pick her for a KitKat. I can't now, anyway. Ruby made me promise.'

'So? Why don't you just choose her anyway?'

Sam looked stricken. 'I don't know!' She ruffled the dog's ears unhappily. 'Usually I just do whatever I want. If I didn't like you very much, I would just put a slug in your shoe without really thinking about it. Or spiders in your pencil case. Or just kick you in the knickers. But then I didn't really have a lot of friends left by the end of Year Six, so I thought I ought to try being a bit nicer.'

Her chin jerked up, eyes wide. 'I wouldn't do any of that to you,' she added quickly. 'Well, not unless I was very bored or you kicked me in the knickers first. Only . . . why's everything got so difficult? I don't know how to keep up. At school, everyone wears tights now, but I've only got socks, and Mum K doesn't believe in tights, and Mum Gen's are all woolly with holes in the toes, so I can't pinch hers. I used to not care about any of that stuff. I *liked* not caring. I was really good at it too. But . . .'

'I understand,' said Billie, nodding sympathetically. She'd never needed to put a slug in someone's shoe; Yasmeen and Mia mostly did as they were told without her needing to. And she had tights: Dad had bought a five-pack of navy ones from Asda. And she still didn't care, mostly, because she was actually brilliant, and other people were just stupid and annoying if they didn't notice.

But last night she'd spent an hour in front of the mirror, wondering if she could use Raffy's razor to make her eyebrows look thinner. She'd tried a bit, in the middle. It still itched.

Maybe Michael was right. Big School was different for girls.

'Year Seven,' she said, with a sigh.

'Yeah!' said Sam feelingly. 'Stupid Year Seven. Stupid being eleven, and a girl, and all of it. '

They both sat sadly on the bed, contemplating the awfulness of it all.

'You know, a *real* friend would want you to do whatever Hero project you liked,' Billie said casually, looking up at the wall of posters.

Sam narrowed her eyes. Then she dashed out of the room, sprinted downstairs, and returned clutching a laptop covered in superhero stickers.

'Would you like to watch Marta's top ten best goals on the internet?' she said, all in rush.

'I would,' said Billie.

It wasn't entirely true. Billie thought football was a bit boring, actually. But being friends with Sam wasn't going to be boring at all.

Hi Mum,

I'm in church so you should definitely be able to hear me. (The new one, not the old one with all the stained glass you used to go to. You know that, though.)

I wonder what watching over us is really like. Are we like TV? Do you change the channel to watch me for a bit, and then switch over when I'm doing something boring like Maths or sleeping or Dad's combing out my hair, and watch Gabriel for a bit instead? Is there Heavenly iPlayer for if you miss something important?

Anyway, I hope you're watching over Raffy an awful lot because Abdelrahman's mate Dev's taxi company is giving him a job on the radio telling taxis where to go, and Raffy once got lost just in Kilburn Co-Op, so he might need some angelic satnav.

Gabriel's coming for dinner tonight and we're having curry and rotis.

Not that I'm thinking about curry and taxis instead of sins, etc. I'm thinking about you and you're in Heaven, so that is pretty holy already.

I wish church was shorter and not boring. You could tell God that – I think he ought to know.

Also please tell God, sorry about Dad falling asleep and snoring in the middle of 'All Things Bright and Beautiful'. He does work really hard. You could tell God to send him some extra sleep and a day off too – that would be nice.

Lots of love,
Amen,
Bye

That night Billie almost skipped as she pulled the tables into place, rearranged all the chairs and fetched the big tablecloth.

The Splendide never opened on Sundays, except for guests – so that just meant Gabriel, really.

That was the best thing about having three brothers – she should have told Dr Paget: having one properly grown-up one who didn't really feel like a brother at all. He was a sort of extra uncle, or half a dad, who never ate your pudding or left foam in the sink, because you didn't see him often enough. But when you did, it was the best.

Billie set up candles, dimmed the lights, put the bashed-up old CD player on shuffle, and sat in the dark, waiting.

There was a roar outside, then a squeal as a flashy yellow sports car jerked to a halt, right outside.

'They're here!' she yelled to the boys in the kitchen, and pulled the door open eagerly.

'Having a power cut?' asked Gabriel in his soft voice, sweeping her into a hug. His hair was shaved down in a perfect fade, and he felt skinny, like always, but warm in his soft wool coat. He smelled nice too; spice and sugar, like the Trini black cake Dad made at Christmas.

'No – I just thought candles would be pretty,' she explained, suddenly doubtful.

'So they are,' said Alexei, striding past Gabriel to hug her too. 'Like you, princess.'

Alexei was Gabriel's boyfriend – a proper one, with kissing and living together. He was tall and charming, handsome in a bony sort of way, with very blond hair and a thick Ukrainian accent (though it sounded just like Russian to everyone else). He was also very rich. The sporty yellow car was his, and their fancy flat in Canary Wharf, and you could just sort of tell by looking at him. He even smelled expensive. But Gabriel liked him, so Billie did too.

'We having a power cut?' said Dad, grinning as he brought out the big steaming dish of curry chicken with potato.

'No, I just . . .' mumbled Billie.

But Dad gave her an understanding wink as he hugged Gabriel.

He shook Alexei's hand, a little stiffly. 'Alexei.'

'Charlie. Good to see you. This all smells so great.'

Michael carried in a pile of dhal puri roti – flat rounds of bread, all wrapped up in a cloth to keep warm. Raffy followed with warm plates. Then they all sat down – Billie had already slipped into the best chair, next to Gabriel – and Dad said grace: a long rambly one with verses in.

'Any of this come home from the warehouse stuffed up your jumper, Raff?' asked Gabriel, smiling as he scooped thick brown curry onto his plate.

Billie gave Gabriel a quick kick on the ankle.

Dad coughed.

'I've moved on, career-wise,' said Raffy. 'Vegetable redistribution – it's not for me.'

Gabriel nodded slowly. 'I could keep an eye out for you, at work. See if there's something that might suit you, a bit more long-term . . .'

Gabriel worked for a charity for homeless

youth, finding them flats and showers and lending them a tie for job interviews. Billie knew he must be really good at it, even if Dad said it paid in pence, not pounds. If she was a homeless youth, she'd want someone like him to help, all calm and peaceful.

But Raffy shook his head once, firm. 'No thanks.'

The table went quiet; just the sound of scraping spoons.

'All this . . . this is excellent, Charlie,' said Alexei, waving a piece of roti. 'You should put this on the menu, huh? Make this place a little restaurant?'

It was Gabriel's turn to cough – and if Billie had been a bit nearer, she might have kicked Alexei on the ankle too, even though you probably weren't supposed to do that with people who weren't your brother. That was what Dad had always wanted: a Trinidadian restaurant. There was always a dish on the menu on Saturdays: pelau rice, Trini callaloo; Jamaican jerk chicken with rice and peas. But it turned out that Kensal Rise mostly liked fry-ups and cheese sandwiches, so that was what

The Splendide mostly sold. It was still a bit of a sore point.

Dad smiled anyway. 'Maybe one day, eh?'

And then it went quiet again. Everyone stared at their plates.

'Stop being weird!' said Billie, wanting to kick them all. 'There's loads to talk about! Like, for example, I have just started Big School, which is quite important and interesting, actually!'

'I have something in the car that will maybe cheer things up, huh? I fetch.' Alexei twinkled his eyes at Billie, the café door tinkling as he stepped outside.

While he was gone, Gabriel asked her lots of questions about Big School, and she told him – about sad Mr Miller, and the two Sams living just down the road, and her Hero project – and he said it was a brilliant idea and would definitely win the competition, which just went to prove he was the very best big brother.

When Alexei came back, he was holding a heavy green bottle.

'Champagne?' said Dad, hurrying to fetch glasses from behind the counter. 'We celebrating?'

Gabriel smiled proudly and put his arm round Alexei's shoulders. 'We are. As of this week, you are looking at a British citizen.'

'God save the Queen, I hate the French, lovely jubbly!' said Alexei. 'Cheers!'

He popped the bottle open, though it didn't spray everywhere like in films; just bubbled out into a glass and fizzed up to the top right away.

Billie was given a small one, just to taste. It was all froth, like when you slurp a can of lemonade right after opening it, but with a distinct aftertaste of poison. One mouthful was definitely enough.

Michael sniffed his glass suspiciously as the bubbles popped in his face. 'So. Um. What does that mean?'

Alexei explained that after living here for seven years he'd been able to apply for citizenship – once he'd passed a test to prove he'd turned a bit British and knew how to queue.

'He gets to vote now – which is pretty scary, what with him being Tory scum and all,' said Gabriel. 'And he gets a fancy purple passport.'

'One thing that is very important: I get to go home to visit Ukraine, and come back with no troubles, so I can see all my family again. It has been a long time. I miss a lot.'

Gabriel squeezed Alexei's hand.

Billie wasn't sure if he meant he missed them a lot, or had missed a lot. But they were the same, really. Dad clinked glasses with Alexei, giving him a nod of understanding.

'But . . . it means one more important thing also,' said Alexei. He coughed and put his glass down. Then he took both Gabriel's hands in his big pale ones.

'Gabriel. I wanted to do this before, as soon as we could. But . . . this citizenship, I need to do that first, just for me. So now it's done. And now I do the thing for us.'

Gabriel's eyes opened wide as Alexei stepped back, dropped down on one knee and pulled a small square box out of his jeans pocket.

'No way,' whispered Michael.

'Bruv,' murmured Raffy.

Alexei flipped the box open. There wasn't a sparkly diamond in there – which was good, Billie thought, because Gabriel wasn't into sparkly diamonds; he didn't even like that bit in *Snow*

White where Dopey puts them in his eyes. There were two plain gold rings instead. One each.

'Gabriel Earl Bright, will you marry me?'

Gabriel didn't say anything, and for an awful moment Billie thought he might not say yes and she'd have to take him outside and tell him off – but it was only because his mouth had gone all quivery. Eventually he made a big sniffly noise, and nodded, and pressed his forehead against Alexei's.

Alexei put one ring on Gabriel's finger. Gabriel managed to get the other out of the box, but he was so trembly he couldn't get it to line up with Alexei's finger. In the end Raffy had to hold his arm steady, and guide it into place.

Then they had a huge snog. Massive. Michael's eyebrows lifted, then dropped thoughtfully.

'Dad?' Gabriel's voice was very soft, and slightly hopeful.

Dad had stood perfectly still through it all, watching, soundless.

But now he gripped them both by the shoulders.

'Aw, my boys. Gabriel. If your mum could see you now . . .'

He glanced at the others. Raffy looked at his shoes.

'She can,' said Billie, kicking the table leg for emphasis. 'I keep telling you. She's watching over us, all the time.'

'Welcome to the family, Alexei.'

Alexei put out his hand to shake, but Dad gave him a big hug instead.

'So, now for the really important question,' said Gabriel, pouring out more champagne and looking from Raffy to Michael to Billie. 'Which one of you wants to be bridesmaid?'

CHAPTER

10

Billie couldn't wait to tell Ruby all about her weekend. (Her brother was getting married, and to a large tattooed Ukrainian, and she was going to be a bridesmaid, which was definitely three interesting and surprising things.)

But Ruby wasn't there.

'Do you think she's ill?' asked Efe on the way to Mr Miller's classroom. 'Like, *ill* ill?'

'She did say she liked cemeteries and tragical things. Not that I think she's, like, *that* ill,' Billie added swiftly. 'Just that she might enjoy being reclined on a bed, coughing.'

Sam sniffed. 'I suppose. Or she's decided she doesn't like us and has gone back to her old school.'

'Can you do that? Just go back to Year Six?' Efe's eyes were suddenly enormous with longing.

Billie knew what she meant. She liked Miss Eagle, and wearing a tie, and getting to melt things in Science. But she missed her old playground with the painted wooden pencils on the fence, and her old teacher, Miss Schofield, who wore wood-block necklaces and played the guitar and was definitely not Eeyore.

They all knew you couldn't go back really; everyone would, and they'd have to write a letter to an alien telling them Big School was shut as no one ever made it to Year 8 at all.

Ruby wasn't there again the next day.

On Wednesday she came back – with a black ribbon tied around one arm, and a whole box of tissues tucked under the other.

'My rabbit,' she sniffed. 'Remington. Poor, tragic Remington. I found her in her hutch on Monday morning, all stiff, so I couldn't possibly come to school. We held the funeral yesterday. It was very moving. I played the violin.'

Then she started crying. Right there in the playground, by the bins.

Billie gave her one of her tightest hugs, the kind she usually saved for Gabriel.

Then Ruby distributed ribbons to all of them, and they wore them all day, taking turns to hold

Ruby's tissue box in case she became overwhelmed with grief in the middle of PE.

At the end of the week it was time for them to choose their Hero projects.

That day Miss Eagle wore a muddy green felt skirt that curved out round her bottom, and a white blouse with pockets. Her hair was twisted up into a roll on top of her head, with the back curling onto her shoulders.

'You look like you should be in a war, miss,' said Big Mohammad. 'But, like, a sexy war.'

'Thank you,' said Miss Eagle eventually. 'I think. But . . . perhaps next time think about where you are before you speak, hmm?'

'I will do that, miss. Cheers,' said Big Mohammad.

Miss Eagle had moved all the tables to one side, and the chairs were in a circle with a gap at the top. Billie sat down with everyone else, her palms feeling sweaty, hugging a precious parcel to her chest, wrapped in a scarf. The 'Heroes!' wall display now had shiny gold paper stapled round the edges, and there were already some pictures pinned up from the other classes: Captain America; Buzz Lightyear; lots of footballers.

There were a few Jessica Ennis-Hills too. Billie glanced at Ruby, who was sitting next to her. Her hair was sticking up at the back, as if it hadn't been brushed that morning. There was a blob of something on her skirt too. She scratched at it anxiously when she saw Billie looking.

Sam, meanwhile, was fiddling with her socks, looking nervous.

Billie wasn't nervous. She couldn't wait. Her picture wouldn't be like anyone else's. That was why she'd stand out, and standing out was always best.

'Now, I hope everyone has their homework prepared,' said Miss Eagle. 'I want each of you to stand up and share with the class who you've chosen to be your hero, and tell us a little bit about why. I'll go first.'

She reached over to her desk, and held up a laminated photograph, black and white, of an Indian woman in military uniform.

'Do any of you know who this is?'

'Is she from the sexy war, miss?'

'See me at the end of the lesson, Mohammad. No one? That's a shame, though it's not all that surprising; no one told me about her when I was at school either. This is Noor Inayat Khan. This photograph was taken in 1941, and she was in *a* war: the Second World War. Noor was part of the Special Operations Executive – one of a select group of incredibly brave women and men who worked undercover as spies, in Occupied France, to send back vital information to the British war effort. Her work saved hundreds of lives. She was awarded the George Cross, and she died in 1944 – executed by the Nazis. She's my hero because she didn't give up. She did what was right, even if it was dangerous. I like to imagine that if I were in her shoes, I would act with that sort of clear-minded courage. I'm not sure I'd be brave enough. But it's something to aspire to. So she's my hero: Noor Inayat Khan.'

Someone started to clap, so they all clapped. Miss Eagle pinned the picture to the wall with a smile.

'Now, that's the sort of thing I'd like to hear from each of you, yes? Some facts, and some personal reasons too. Remember to speak slowly and clearly, and to project your voice so we can all hear you. Everyone happy?'

7E were not happy. 7E were mostly wishing they'd picked a real-life amazing dead spy lady, not a made-up man in a spider costume.

But it was too late. Miss Eagle went to the back of the room and perched on a table, holding a clipboard to make notes.

Halid went first, holding up a very crumpled poster of Amir Khan, the boxer.

'He's got medals and a belt and loads of prize money. And he trains really hard but is kind to animals.'

Miss Eagle nodded. 'What else about him do you admire, Halid?'

'Um. I admire how he eats two whole chickens a day. Because I really like chicken.'

Everyone clapped as he sat down.

Nishat read out a little essay about her uncle Prasad, who worked as a doctor for Médecins Sans Frontières, vaccinating tiny babies.

There was more clapping.

Thor and Iron Man and J. K. Rowling all got pinned to the 'Heroes!' wall.

Then it was Billie's turn.

Billie hadn't made any notes. She didn't need to. She liked speaking in front of an audience; everyone had to be quiet and pay attention just to you. She stood at the front, and said in a clear, loud voice, 'My hero is my mum,' and slowly unwrapped the scarf from round the picture, for maximum dramatic effect.

There was a little ripple around the room, like whispers, or very impressed ghosts.

It was in a frame, with glass, and not a photo or a page cut from a magazine. This was a large drawing on buff-coloured paper, in smudgy charcoal and delicate white chalk, of a pretty, birdlike woman with long wavy hair and a solemn expression, her head lowered to read a book.

'Yeah, right, like that's your mum,' muttered Alfie.

'Not cool, bruv,' whispered Acacia.

'Yeah – don't you know people can be adopted?' snapped Lianne.

'I'm not adopted,' said Billie hotly. 'That's my mum – that's what she looked like.'

Alfie sat up suddenly, his eyes flicking around

the room in horror. 'No! I just – I meant it's a really good drawing. Like from an art gallery. Not, like, racist. Oh my God, I'm not, like, stupid.'

'You are, though, mate,' said Big Mohammad.

'Totally,' said Lianne.

Miss Eagle coughed. 'I think we've strayed a little off the point. Billie – it's a beautiful picture, and worthy of an art gallery, absolutely. It's lovely that you've chosen your mum. Tell us more about her.'

'Well,' said Billie. 'She . . . um . . . Her name was Cariad, which means *darling* in Welsh, because she was from Wales – though her dad was Italian. My brother Gabriel drew this of her when he was at school. He's a really good artist – he could've gone to art college if he wanted but he works for a charity now instead. We keep this picture on the wall in our living room with all our other best photos of her, but this is my favourite. I think she looks really pretty. Like an angel.'

'And what was she like?' prompted Miss Eagle gently.

'Um. She was kind. And brave when she was poorly. And . . . like a really good mum . . .' Billie trailed off.

The clapping took place in a fog as she went back to her seat.

She didn't really register the rest of the lesson: Efe trying to explain why she'd picked Jessica Ennis-Hill when she didn't know who Jessica Ennis-Hill was; Sam standing up with shaky pride and introducing them all to Marta, five times Player of the Year.

When Miss Eagle took her aside at the end, to suggest that Billie took the framed drawing home and brought back a photograph – 'It's irreplaceable, I'd feel dreadful if it got damaged' – she just nodded dumbly, as if she was swimming underwater.

'I don't *mind*,' Ruby was saying to Sam in a tone that said she very much did, as Billie stumbled out into the corridor. 'You could've *said*.'

She left them behind, went to the spidery toilets behind C Block, and locked herself in a cubicle.

She unwrapped the drawing again, and propped it up on her knees.

She touched the glass. It was all so familiar: the rounded curve of the cheek; the strands of hair that fell across the face picked out with white chalk; the solemn, globe-like eyes with their long lashes looking down at something unseen, the expression unreadable. Gabriel swore it was a book in her hands, a book she'd read while sitting for his picture – but Billie had always liked to think it was a baby she was holding. A baby that was her.

Cariad Bright.

What was she like?

I was only five, Billie wanted to say back. *I was only five years old when she went away, and that wasn't really long enough to know, was it?*

She knew what was in the Memory Box stuffed under her bed.

She knew the stories from the funeral: how her mum had waved *The Children's Illustrated Bible* over Billie's cot because Ariel was an angel name, honest; how she had tripped over the hem of her wedding dress, and that's why all the photos were from the knee up so you couldn't see the rip.

She remembered what she smelled like, sort of, if you counted perfume; there was a squarish glass bottle in a drawer in Dad's room, a precious few teaspoonfuls left.

But that didn't add up to a person; not really.

How were you supposed to win a Hero project competition when you didn't know anything about your hero?

Hi Mum,

It is very unfair of you to have gone off and died without bothering to tell me all about you and what you're like. It's for school and everything. If we all have to go to the KYLO REN SPORTS & LEISURE COMPLEX for the rest of our lives, it will be all your fault. And Madison's for picking him.

Well, actually, it's God's for taking you away before I learned all the important things about you. Stupid God.

I so should've picked Jessica Ennis-Hill. At least she's on Wikipedia.

Lots of love,
Amen,
Bye

CHAPTER 11

On the bus home Billie kept her arms wrapped tight and nervous around Gabriel's drawing. She had to sit in the seat behind again – but instead of the swingy-ponytail girl, Michael had a new one snuggled up beside him: light-skinned, candyfloss-pink hair, pale pink lipstick and big hoopy earrings she'd put in at the bus stop.

This one seemed much better at kissing. Every one on the mouth, a bit slurpy, all the way to Sorrel Street – until at the end she ruined it by licking his ear.

(Really, Billie had no idea where these girls were getting their kiss-training from. When she got to the kissing part of growing up, she was going to do it properly.)

When they got off, Michael shuffled his feet as the candyfloss-haired girl blew him kisses through the steamy bus window.

'Kamila. She's. Um. Another friend,' he mumbled, his hands in his pockets.

'Uh-huh,' said Billie. 'So what happened with Natasha?'

'Nothing.'

Billie poked him hard in the stomach. 'Michael! Are you being a horrible cheater?'

'It's not my fault! It's just . . . girls. They sort of . . . like me. And sit next to me. And then they put their tongue in my mouth.'

'Without even asking?' said Billie, incredulous.

'There was no asking,' said Michael weakly, widening his eyes at the memory.

Billie blinked. 'Never mind about all that, I need to ask you a thing,' she said, following him through the peely-paint front door, up the stairs, and plonking herself on the good armchair before he could get there. 'How come we never talk about Mum?'

Michael frowned. 'Um. We do.'

'*I* do. And Dad does sometimes, like on birthdays and Christmas and Picnic Day.'

Picnic Day was the 5th of February. It was her deathday, really, her last day, but no one liked to call it that. They had a well-worn routine: Dad went to put flowers on her grave with anyone who wanted to come, then they had an indoor picnic and watched *Harry Potter and the Prisoner of Azkaban*. (It was her favourite. She liked all the woolly jumpers.)

'Anyway, that's not the sort of talking I mean. I mean, *about* her. Like, about things she did, and what she was like, and the brilliant superheroic kind of person she was.'

'Oh.' Michael scratched his head. 'Um. I could try to do that more. If you want.'

'Go on then.'

He scratched his head again. 'Um. She used to do loads of knitting.'

Billie waited, but Michael just looked at her.

'What? It was a thing she did. She'd sit here on the sofa when *Coronation Street* was on, and do little cardies and stuff. She could do, like, a whole arm before the adverts.'

'Hopeless,' sighed Billie, jumping up. 'No wonder they aren't letting Year Tens do a Hero project. Yours would be rubbish.'

She took Gabriel's drawing up to her room, and propped it up on her desk.

She stared into it for ages. But it didn't magically come to life and start singing a song about feelings, or anything useful, so she went down to The Splendide and sat swinging her legs and staring at Dad with a needy expression until he gave in.

'What happened, angel?' he said, abandoning the queue to Gloria and slipping onto the high stool beside her. 'You in trouble?'

Billie shook her head. 'Nothing happened. I just really need to talk to you. About Mum. Because I'm writing a Hero project about her and I can't make it all about how she was pretty in a drawing and did some knitting. What kind of a role model is that?'

Dad's forehead went crinkly. 'I feel like I came into a conversation in the middle. What is this?'

Billie sighed and explained again, only this time her face went a bit wobbly.

Dad's forehead went even crinklier. Then he rubbed his eyes and darted over to the counter to murmur something to Gloria. When he came back, he was smiling.

'Come on, bright girl. You and me, upstairs. We're on dinner duty.'

'But it's not our turn! And . . .' She waved her

hand at the three tables that had to be cleared; at the two people waiting for coffees.

Dad grabbed her hand and squeezed it. 'You are more important than whatever's down here, I promise.' He checked his watch. 'And if we start it now, there's time for pizza dough to rise . . .'

Billie hopped off her stool at once.

Upstairs, she helped weigh out strong flour and yeast, a dash of sugar, olive oil and a little warm water. Then she watched as her dad swept it all together till it went from sticky lumps glued to his fingers to a warm stretchy dough. He split it in half, and they shared the kneading job, smushing it over and over.

'Did Mum teach you how to make pizza?'

She was Italian, after all. Well, sort of.

But Dad laughed. 'No, sweet girl. Your mama was a lot of things, but she was not a cook.'

'Is that why she married you?'

'Heck no! It's why she nearly didn't.' He frowned down at her. 'You know all this, child. Cilenti's – the ice-cream place by the sea . . . ?'

It sounded a bit familiar.

Dad scooped the two rounds of dough together,

pressing them hard a few more times before dropping them into a bowl, covering it with cling film to keep it warm and help it rise. He scraped all the bits of dough off their hands.

Then he disappeared into the hallway. He came back holding a thick grey photo album, dropped onto the sofa and patted the seat beside him.

The album was full of old photos – of baby Gabriel, and then babies Raffy and Michael with a proud-looking Gabriel standing between them, then baby Billie, who always seemed to have her mouth open. Dad was in a few, looking confusingly unbald and skinny. (They both giggled at those.) Granny was there too in one of the older ones, before Billie was born. (That made Dad pause and run his finger slowly across the faces.) But Mum wasn't there at all, except for one awkward-looking posed picture in a hat, at somebody's wedding.

'Always behind the camera,' Dad muttered, flipping the pages. 'Ah. Here we go.'

Not spread between the pages but tucked into the back cover, there she was. Mum, before she was Mum. Cariad the teenager, with wavy brown hair in a cloud round her head, wearing tiny pink shorts, a billowy white T-shirt that would fit Michael, and a sulk. There was an older boy next to her with his hair in two short curtains parted in the centre, grinning and pointing up with both fingers at the sign above their heads: CILENTI'S.

'Is that . . . Uncle Fed?'

Dad nodded. 'He's put on a few since too,' he added, patting his belly. 'Or he had, last time I saw him. And that's their dad's place, in Barry Island. Takeaway chips and cups of tea for the beach, and tables inside for when it was rainy. Her and Fed used to work there every summer. When she turned eighteen, she said, *Nope, no more, I'm off to London, see you.* Up to the Big Smoke to seek her fortune. Night I met her, she was singing in a pub.'

'So she was going to be a singer?' Billie asked hopefully.

A singer wasn't heroic, exactly. But it was something that could definitely go in a project for school. A fact. A piece of a mum.

Only Dad was smiling, shaking his head. 'Ohhh, no. She was horrible. But *I* thought she was magic, pure magic. Charmed her off the

98

stage and bought her drinks all night like an idiot because that was what the pub paid the performers: two rum and Cokes and a packet of scampi fries. The Three Goats' Heads. No, wait. The Three Horseshoes. No. There was a three in it, I know that.'

'And you fell in love?'

'And we fell in love. Or I did. And I talked her round in the end. She was a beautiful girl, angel. Just like you.' He kissed the top of Billie's head.

She wriggled away. She was old now; she didn't need all that. Even if it was nice.

'You really never heard any of that before, child?'

Billie shook her head. 'Nope. You kind of don't talk about her ever at all.'

Dad blinked slowly, looking tired again all of a sudden. 'I'm sorry. I think we did, when you were littler, and you've forgotten. And . . . well. You know, you come home, you have new things to say. Today, I sold out of Bakewell tarts, when last week I couldn't shift them. Today at school you learned about . . .'

'Um. Prolate spheroids.'

'OK. Today at school you learned about prolate spheroids.' Dad paused, looking worried.

'It's like an egg,' Billie supplied. 'Or a rugby ball.'

'Oh! OK. So, those are the things we end up talking about. But your mum, she didn't do anything new today. So it doesn't come up. You see?'

Billie nodded. 'It's sad,' she said. 'That she didn't get to do anything new today.'

'It is, angel. It is. Maybe that's why we don't talk about her all the time too. Because we don't want to always be sad.'

'Team Bright.'

'Always smiling.' He smiled, slapping the photo album closed. 'You want to grate the cheese or chop the onions?'

Billie picked cheese, obviously, and ate half while watching the dough grow, and grow, and grow.

Hi Mum,

I've decided not knowing anything about you is EXCITING and GOOD and BEST, after all, actually, whoop! Because you are MYSTERIOUS and SECRETIVE, and now I get to be like a detective and investigate you.

Maybe you were some sort of spy or secret agent or an actual superhero with a secret double life as just a mum. That would make a lot of sense. I hope you had a good superhero name like NINJA HARPOON not, like, MUMSY BLIZZARD or WELSHCAKE.

It's OK if you were though, because that would make you a really good person to go on the Heroes! wall display, and then I'll win, and then you will be proud of me. (I was a bit worried Ruby would win and then I'd have to punch her on the nose and I don't think you'd be proud of that.)

I know I asked you to watch over Raffy, but could you watch over Michael a bit more too? Because of all the kissing. I know teenagers are meant to be all sexy these days, but he probably doesn't need to kiss everyone.

I feel like there is a whole new you out there, waiting for me to find her.

She could send a sign to point me in the right direction – that would be fine and not cheating.

Lots of love,

Amen,

Bye

12

After church on Sunday Billie sat at the top of the stairs, tapping her feet, her arms wrapped round a different sort of homework.

At last there was a thrum of an engine and a squeal of tyres.

'I'm off to have brunch and be bridesmaidy!' she yelled, and raced downstairs.

Alexei's yellow car was the sort that only really had two seats, and a tiny space at the back – but she was small enough to just fit in behind Gabriel.

'All set?' he said in his soft voice.

She nodded gleefully, and Alexei put his foot down.

First they drove to the fanciest café Billie had ever been to. The ceilings were high enough it could have actual trees growing in pots indoors, and there were mirrors on all the walls, and French waiters with square white aprons.

'Don't tell Dad,' said Gabriel, winking as he held the door open for her.

(It was a house rule: no cafés. Billie giggled.)

'The French toast, it is to die for,' said Alexei when the menus arrived. 'Trust your Alexei.'

Billie didn't know what French toast was, but it turned out to be eggy bread like Dad sometimes made with stale ends of the loaf – but this kind came with icing sugar, blueberries and syrup. It made her feel very sticky. There was orange juice too, with disgusting bits in, but she held her nose and drank it anyway.

Then Alexei drove them back to the flat.

Canary Wharf was a long way on the Jubilee line, so Billie had only been there once before, for a pre-Christmas party. It was even shinier than she remembered: all chrome and glass, with a lift up to the sixth floor like in a shopping mall just to get there. All the walls were white, and the sofa (which did not squish you together comfily when you sat on it; it was very firm) was stiff white leather – but there were bright green cushions and a bright green rug, and all the kitchen things were bright green too: the kettle, and the handles of the knives and forks. There was a balcony too, looking out over the mud-grey Thames, the London Eye just visible.

It wasn't cosy. It wasn't somewhere you could spill any Vimto at all. It was like being in a film of London, not the real one. But Billie thought it was very nice to visit.

They all sat on the white sofa, and Alexei opened another bottle of champagne.

'For good luck!' he said, pressing a glass into Gabriel's hand.

'We don't always drink champagne, Bills,' Gabriel whispered, holding it awkwardly. 'I mean – I'd have been fine with a cup of tea, babe.'

Alexei rolled his eyes and tapped their glasses together with a bright *ting*.

'Never mind about that,' said Billie, sliding forward on the uncomfy sofa. 'I've done a lot of bridesmaiding homework and research, and I can't help you with the usual stuff like doing up the buttons on your dress, or fixing your hair, or taking you out to a big drunk party full of hens and people wearing pink sashes.'

'Yeah, let's skip all that,' said Gabriel with a smile.

'Good. So I thought I should be helpful with everything else. This was one pound fifty in the charity shop, which was *all* my pocket money, but you don't have to pay me back. Call it an early wedding present.'

She reached into her Tiny Robot Unicorn Friends backpack and pulled out *Your Big Day: 101 Essentials for Every Wedding Planner*. It already had sticky Post-its everywhere, where she'd marked the most important things.

Gabriel's eyebrows lifted.

'I knew we asked the right one, huh?' said Alexei, grinning as he nudged Gabriel's arm. 'You will make a very good *druzhka*.'

Billie glowed, feeling proud (even though she didn't know what a *druzhka* was). But Gabriel twisted his hands together. 'Did the boys mind, do you think?' he asked Billie. 'Not being asked to be, like, a best man or something?'

Billie shook her head. 'Michael's really busy with . . . training. And Raffy's busy with . . . being Raffy. I bet they don't.'

Raffy wasn't that busy, actually. The taxi job hadn't worked out ('How was I supposed to know that there's a Kennington *and* a Kensington? That's just, like, bad city planning'), so he was waiting for Dev's mate Subra to call him back about some night shifts cleaning offices in the city. But she thought he might not want her to tell Gabriel.

She glowed inside a little at knowing things he didn't. At keeping secrets like the best, most grown-up little sister ever.

'And I'll be really good at it, I promise. Look, the book has all the main decisions.'

She opened it and ran her finger down the list on page 4. *'Location of ceremony.'*

'Some churches, they would marry us now . . . ?' said Alexei.

'Register office,' said Gabriel firmly.

Billie made a note on a new Post-it. *'Location of wedding reception.'*

'Big!' said Alexei. 'A castle! An aquarium!'

'Or small – small would be fine,' said Gabriel.

'Number of guests.'

'It's a party. Everyone!'

'Or we could just keep it to a few friends – close family,' said Gabriel.

Billie went on through the list.

Catering.

Cake.

Flowers.

Photographer.

Rings.

Suit hire.

Gift list.

'No-no-no, this is no good,' said Alexei, taking the book and flipping through the pages. 'This is all on one day? There's only one meal? And . . . where are the horses?'

'Horses?' said Gabriel faintly.

'Horses, yes. In Ukraine – in western Ukraine, we are more traditional, not so Russian – we always have horses. Horses, and two days of wedding, and live band, and three tables for the food. It is not a wedding without.'

About the only thing they agreed on was the date.

'December the twelfth,' they said in unison.

'Anniversary of our first date,' explained Gabriel, smiling. 'And I thought it could be kind of Christmassy. White lights . . . white flowers . . . Alexei could wear those fluffy white ear muffs that make him look mental . . .'

'Ice sculptures!' said Alexei. 'And there must be snow. If no snow, we hire a snow machine.'

Billie flipped through the pages of the wedding book. 'Oh,' she said. 'It says here that you should start planning eighteen months to two years before the ceremony. And December's only . . . three months away.'

Gabriel groaned, and dropped his head back onto the white leather.

'So – we hire a real wedding planner, like I said,' said Alexei, furrowing his brow. 'You are very magical, Billie – I like this book, I like your brains – but you know, someone to do all these decisions for us. Take away the worries. Find us the *horses*.' He gripped Gabriel's hand intently, squeezing it tight.

Gabriel glanced at Billie apologetically. 'Maybe I will have that cup of tea,' he said, and disappeared into the kitchen.

Alexei grumbled, then rooted around in his coat pocket for a cigarette. He went out onto the balcony, blowing smoke into the rain.

Billie chewed her bottom lip. She knew what the problem was. Gabriel didn't like fuss. He didn't even like having his photo taken. He liked quiet, and home, and donating things to Oxfam. He definitely didn't want a two-day sort of wedding with horses and a snow machine, even if there was time to arrange one.

But if she knew that, why didn't Alexei?

Billie gathered a bright green blanket from the back of the sofa around herself and joined Alexei, leaning against the balcony rail, trying not to cough when his smoke blew in her face.

'Um,' she said eventually. 'Alexei? I totally like your ideas, but I think Gabriel wants a wedding that's sort of less . . . weddingy.'

Alexei sighed. 'I know. Silly boy.' He turned and flashed Billie a grin. 'He'll come round, you'll see. It's going to be his best day ever.'

Billie watched the little ferryboats going up and down on the muddy brown water as Alexei told her about the dress his mother had already bought, and his aunts, who had already booked their flights, and all the traditions he loved best: *korovai*, which was a kind of bread; the *brama*,

where the groom comes to the bride's gates and
his friends try to show that he is worthy; his hands
waving wildly, his eyes bright and happy.

When he'd finished his cigarette, she gave him
a big hug, tight round his middle.

'Best day ever,' she whispered into his shirt.

She was his bridesmaid too, after all.

Hi Mum,

Do you know how to have a small wedding that's also a big wedding at the same time? Like, instead of a reception in an aquarium, maybe we could just have crisps around a fish tank. And instead of horses, we could just have Sam's dog, so long as it is on a lead and doesn't come too close.

I asked Dad if there were any Trini traditions we should do as well, but he just sniffed and said, 'I've offered my help; they know where I am if they decide they want it.'

I think he means money. In my wedding planning book it says that the father of the bride traditionally pays for the wedding – but Raffy said that's from the Olden Days when women were like property and you married them to get their camels. Or something. Anyway, there isn't a bride. And Alexei's definitely got more money than Dad, or Gabriel, so it makes sense for him to pay for things. But when I told Dad that, he dropped a ham-and-cheese toastie on the floor, so I don't think he understands about it not being the Olden Days any more.

If you were here, I bet you would know what to

say better than me, and then it would be fixed. Not to make you feel bad or anything.

I'll work it out.

Gabriel said, however big the wedding ends up, I'm allowed to invite one friend. I don't know who to pick, though. I think Sam would be the most fun. But I think she wouldn't mind if I asked Efe instead. But then Ruby will want it to be her, obviously, and will be mean if it isn't. Alexei said I could bring a boyfriend if I wanted, though – and then Gabriel said, 'Or a girlfriend – don't assume,' and now I'm a bit worried. I like being old and grown up, but I don't want to have to put my tongue in anyone's mouth, whether they're a boy or a girl. And I can't imagine I am ever going to like someone enough to lick their ear.

A sign to help me choose who to take would be good. Don't poo on anyone, though, 'cos then they might not want to come at all.

Lots of love,
Amen,
Bye

CHAPTER
13

Monday morning brought two surprises.

First, Big Mohammad sprinted right through the middle of Billie, Sam and Efe in the yard, almost knocking them over, his face all blotchy and a dirty wet splodge down his white shirt.

A pigeon had pooed on his shoulder.

'It's lucky, bruv, shut up,' he yelled sulkily as Halid and Alfie ran after him, laughing.

Billie hid her face in her wedding planner book, and tried not to think about angelic signs or Big Mohammad's tongue.

'Why are you reading *that*?' asked Ruby, marching up and wrinkling her nose. There was a blob on her clothes again, as if they hadn't been washed at the weekend; this time on her sleeve, red like ketchup.

Billie ignored the blob, and explained all about Gabriel and Alexei getting married. (She missed out the part with the horses.)

'We haven't got very long to organize it, though. In my book it says if you need an emergency, very quick, instant wedding, you can phone round and see if anyone decided not to get married after all and buy theirs off them for cheap. All you need to do is scrape the names off the cake and ice new ones on. But I don't think Alexei would fancy that.'

'Well, either way it'll be *fah*-bulous,' said Ruby. 'Gay weddings always are.'

'Have you ever been to one?' asked Sam.

Ruby flicked her hair crossly. 'No. But everyone knows that.'

Sam shrugged. 'My mums didn't get married. Mum Gen wanted to get Civil Partnered, when that was a thing, but Mum K said weddings are society's way of making you spend five hundred quid on a cake, which Mum Gen said sort of took the romance out of it really.'

'I'm never getting married,' said Efe gloomily. 'You have to get divorced again afterwards, and then everything is yelling over who owns the sofa. I don't want any of that.'

'You get presents, though,' said Ruby.

'Not nice stuff. Mostly plates.'

'When my cousin got married, she asked for an Xbox,' said Sam thoughtfully. 'But no one gave it to her. It was totally mostly plates.'

'Well, I'm definitely getting married,' said Ruby, flicking her hair again. 'But not until I'm twenty-five so I can be well-established in my career first. I'm going to wear ivory lace, not white, because I'm original. We're going to have three children. Two girls and a boy. And a part-time nanny to help me maintain my work–life balance.'

'Um. I don't think it works like that,' said Sam.

Ruby shook her head. 'It does if you plan carefully and focus on your goals. You have to have a Life List. You write down your Life List of what you want out of life on a piece of a paper, and then it comes true. My mum's got a book all about it.'

Sam made a little snorty noise. Ruby's eyes narrowed.

'Are you going to get married one day?' Efe asked Billie.

Billie frowned. Why did everyone suddenly want her to kiss people and get married?

Ruby leaned close to Billie, her head tilting sympathetically as she patted Billie's hand.

'Of course, you do have to find someone willing to marry you first,' she said.

Billie closed up the book with a snap.

The second surprise arrived in Mr Miller's classroom, in brown envelopes. There was a pile of them on his desk, and he began to pass them out, while sighing.

'Our esteemed head teacher Mrs Cooper has, it appears, finally misplaced her last marble and taken it upon herself to interfere in your lives *outside* school – and mine too. But not hers. No, she'll be at home putting her feet up. Of course. It says here . . .' Mr Miller read from a sheet of paper. '*To encourage our new young students to build a strong sense of school and community spirit and help them settle into the challenging environment of secondary education, we are pleased to announce . . . the Special Sevens Sleepover.*'

He paused to groan in despair.

'*This is an overnight stay, fully supervised, at the beginning of the half-term holiday. It is not an educational event and not compulsory, but we encourage your child's*

117

attendance. This year, due to the building works on site, we are delighted to announce a special venue for the sleepover, in association with the Arts Council and Museums of London, at a fully discounted rate. The sleepover will take place at the Natural History Museum in central London!' He paused, looking up. 'There is an exclamation mark there – I haven't just suddenly mutated into someone who cares. *This is*, it says, *a once-in-a-lifetime opportunity to sleep inside this historic building, in the company of our giant blue whale, or the world-famous skeleton of Dippy the dinosaur.* And me. And Miss Eagle and Mrs Shah, who have the deep and joyous privilege of supervising the bloody thing.

'Ahem. Places on the sleepover are limited. You need to take these letters home. Get the slip inside signed and returned to me BY FRIDAY. Any student who does not return a signed slip WILL BE EXCLUDED. No exceptions.'

At lunch, it was all anyone could talk about.

'My mum'll definitely say yes,' said Ruby eagerly. 'She thinks it's very important for me to participate in all school activities.'

Sam snorted. 'Like anyone's going to say no!

118

It's like a parental night off. My mums'll be like naughty teenagers left unsupervised. We'll get back in the morning and find they've trashed the place with, like, literature and fine cheeses.'

Efe looked less certain. 'Is it everyone? All of Year Seven . . . all . . . sleeping together?'

'That *would* be an educational event,' said Ruby smirkily, twirling her leftover takeaway noodles.

'No – I mean – like, all in the same room, kind of . . .' Efe said, her voice trailing off.

'I always thought it would be cool to be in a museum at night,' said Sam, peeling a banana. 'Have you been there? It's well spooky. And it'll nearly be Halloween. We can dress up! And we might see, like, the ghost of a dinosaur.'

Efe looked like she might climb under the table.

'Only we won't because ghosts aren't real,' said Billie quickly. 'It's OK, Efe. You can put your sleeping bag next to mine. I don't get nervous about anything.'

Ruby stared at her crossly, as if she wished she'd thought of saying that first.

It turned out that Efe had never been on a sleep-over before, and sometimes had funny dreams, and thought that the whole school knowing you had funny dreams probably wouldn't be a very good thing – which, if Billie was being entirely honest, was true.

'You just need a practice go,' said Billie confidently. 'Come and stay at my flat one night before it happens. There's a spare bed in my bedroom so you wouldn't even need a sleeping bag. My dad'll make us breakfast in the café in the morning. The bacon baps are really good. And the hot chocolate.'

Sam nodded. 'My mums go there all the time now they know it isn't just a dodgy greasy spoon that gives you food poisoning. Hey! I could come too – I only live down the road.'

There was an awkward pause while Ruby twirled her noodles noisily round in their box.

Sam looked at Efe.

Efe looked at Billie.

Billie looked at the ketchuppy blob on Ruby's sleeve.

'Um . . .' she began to say.

But Ruby looked up, sniffing airily. 'I'm sure your little sleepover thingy will be very sweet, but my weekends are always *very* busy. And I don't need to practise *going to sleep.*' She rolled her eyes and stalked off to fill up her NutriGenix water bottle.

'Who says you were even invited?' muttered Sam under her breath.

Billie felt a little tingle of guilt. Team Bright didn't leave people out; not even annoying ones with ketchup on their sleeves. But there wasn't really space for four people in her bedroom anyway, she decided. It was all for the best.

CHAPTER 14

On Saturday, when Billie went down to the café for her bacon bap, the Paget-Skidelskys were already there.

'Look, angel – my new favourite customers, back again!' said Dad, smiling broadly as he refilled their coffee cups.

'We couldn't resist,' said Dr Paget. 'Sam's been looking forward to his cheese baguette all week, haven't you?'

The boy Sam nodded, chewing happily.

Billie noted the small dog sitting curled up at his feet, and she perched on a stool at a safe distance beside Sam, who was inhaling a ham and tomato one in huge crumby bites.

'Year Seven clearly doesn't spoil the appetite,' said Dr Skidelsky, watching her in mild alarm.

The boy Sam shook his head. 'Everyone said Big School was all hard Geography and being wedgied in the boys' toilets, but it's not those all the time. Not in Miss Eagle's class, anyway. You still get to do a tiny bit of cutting and sticking.'

They all gave a sigh of mourning for the days of full-time cutting and sticking.

'How's your Hero project coming along, Billie?' asked Dr Paget.

'Um,' said Billie.

To be honest, it wasn't. She'd done a cover coloured in with lots of silver pen, with a drawing of Mum's face copied from Gabriel's. (It wasn't as good as his, because she only had pencils, not proper smudgy charcoal; she'd tried burning some toast to see if that would do, but it just tore holes in the paper and made Michael hungry.) Inside, the pages were all still blank. It turned out that 'wore pink shorts in a photo' and 'horrible singer at a pub whose name Dad can't remember' were no more heroic than knitting and being pretty.

'Let's work on ours together,' said Sam. 'But at your house, not ours, because Mum K made chocolate cake with secret aubergines in, and it's not polite to poison your friends with stealthy vegetables.' She eyed the sticky pecan pie on the café counter meaningfully.

There was a brief argument – in which Dr Skidelsky maintained that aubergines were delightful, and Dr Paget tried to suggest that the boy Sam came too – until he claimed to have project-writing plans with a person called Pea (really, Billie thought, he could've just said no – or thought of an imaginary friend with a name anyone might actually believe in). Then Dad came and Splendided at them till it was all agreed.

Billie led Sam up the stairs into her little attic bedroom, carrying two slices of pie in a paper bag and feeling excited. It was always best having friends round to your own house, because you got to tell them what to do, and also there wasn't a dog.

Sam gazed around the walls, wrinkling her nose critically. 'Big Disney fan, huh?'

There were a few posters, and all her DVDs on a shelf, and the soundtracks on CD, and a row of books, and her princesses bedspread.

Billie was about to say, *Yes, obviously, they are the best stories and I will fight you if you don't like them.*

But Sam shrugged, and flopped onto the bed. 'Hey, I like a footballer no one's ever heard of. At least you've got company.'

So Billie put the *Little Mermaid* music on in the background, and hummed along while adding more silver pen to her project's front cover.

'You must have *something* to write about,' said Sam, turning over all the empty pages with a frown. 'I mean . . . she was your mum. Mums do loads of stuff. Mine do anyway.'

'She definitely did. Only we don't talk about her much, because she doesn't do anything new, like learning about prolate spheroids.'

'Maybe she left a secret diary behind,' suggested Sam. 'Or letters! People do that, don't they? Leave letters if they know they're going to die. They do in films.'

'She *did* leave letters. But mine's for, like, a five-year-old. It just says I'm going to grow up to be a beautiful young woman and *spread my wings.*'

Sam looked vomity. Then she brightened. 'We should go on the internet! There's stuff about everyone there, Mum K says, and none of it ever really gets deleted, which is why you should never take a selfie of yourself in your pants. Where's your laptop? Or iPad or whatever?'

Billie shook her head. 'Haven't got one.'

There was an elderly computer in the café, in the tiny cupboardlike office off the kitchen, where Dad stayed up till gone midnight sometimes, scratching his head over spreadsheets. But none of them was allowed in there.

'We can look on your phone then.'

Billie's phone was a bit like the elderly computer compared to Sam's, so they used hers.

Googling *Cariad Bright* only brought up a handful of pages, all about camping shops in Wales, and fancy lovespoons.

'Try *Cariad Cilenti* – that was her name before she married my dad.'

That brought up no one at all.

They tried looking for Uncle Fed, but *Federico Cilenti* brought up lots of Italians: real people on Twitter and Facebook. They clicked on a few and looked at their photos, but it felt a bit nosy and strange; like pressing your face up against someone's window while they were inside watching telly. (Billie hadn't seen him in years, and didn't mind much; she had a vague memory of him picking her up and twirling her round on his shoulders before he'd even said hello.)

Even looking up *Cilenti's* in Barry Island was no use; it was now a Costa Coffee. (Billie decided not to mention that to Dad.)

'Wow. There isn't stuff about everyone on the internet after all,' said Sam wonderingly. 'She's like a proper mystery woman, your mum.'

Billie felt stomach-flippy. The chances of Mum being a spy, or a secret agent, or actually a superhero with an amazing double life shot up by a million per cent to an actual real possibility. *Sorry, Jessica Ennis-Hill,* she thought, *but that is better than a load of gold medals and I am totally going to win the Hero project.*

Sam seemed to think so too. 'Have you got any of her stuff, still? There might be, you know, *clues.*'

She did. Her attic bedroom was where everything that didn't fit anywhere else lived – in big cupboards rising up to the ceiling all along one wall. Billie stood on a chair and opened the top one.

Mum's wedding dress was up there, she knew,

in a zipped-up plastic bag: long, slippery white silk with a trail of tiny pink and red roses winding down one sleeve, and a tiny rip at the hem. There was Dad's wedding suit too, and their photo album: a heavy white cover with *Charles & Cariad: Our Special Day* printed on it in gold. There were boxes of boring files: payslips and paperwork, certificates in envelopes. And, wedged right at the back, there was a suitcase.

It was brown leather, in a sort of snakeskin pattern, with a gold zip.

Billie set it down on the floor and sat in front of it. 'Was it your mum's?'

She stroked her hand across the dusty, bumpy surface, and nodded.

It was. She remembered it vaguely. It was as if she'd known it was there, somehow; as if it had waited till she really needed it. Like a sign.

She opened the zip, held her breath and flipped up the lid.

'Oh,' said Sam, disappointed. 'It's just clothes.'

There was a woolly cardigan Mum had made herself, grey with yellow lemons knitted into it, bobbly from being worn, and holey from her being not especially good at knitting. There were her favourite pyjamas, with snowflakes and reindeers all over. There was a pair of new slippers, still fluffy on the inside.

Under the clothes was a carefully arranged collection of small also-loved things: a cloth bag of knitting needles and wool; a book (romantic-looking, with a shoe and a hedge on the cover); a photo in a glittery frame of all the family by a Christmas tree; and a jewellery box containing a heavy silver charm bracelet jumbled up with a few rings and gold chains.

It was her hospice case, Billie realized; the bag she'd packed for her last week of still being alive. All her most comforting things. Billie touched each one once, reverently, like a spell. She picked up the cardigan and rubbed it against her cheek.

'Do you want me to leave you alone?' whispered Sam.

Billie shook her head. It was nice, having an audience for the big moment. She felt like a girl in a film, about to discover that she had magical ice fingers that made everything snowy, or a mermaid about to grow legs.

'What's that?' said Sam, poking a large bump in the lining.

There was an extra pocket in the lid of the case, with an elasticated edge to hold things in tight. Billie slid her hand inside and felt something cool and metallic.

It was a box. Like a cash box: solid, about the same size as the jewellery box but plain grey and much heavier.

It rattled when she shook it.

Billie felt a tingle walk up her spine. This was it.

She pressed the catch, sliding the little silver button across.

It wouldn't open.

Sam tried hitting it on the edge of the suitcase, and the bed, and the wooden handle of the wardrobe.

'It's locked,' she said eventually.

Billie peered at the catch. There was a tiny keyhole, shaped like a perfect circle with a notch underneath. But there was no key – not in the silky pocket of the case, or tucked into the cardigan or the pages of the book.

'We could try picking the lock,' suggested Sam, brandishing a knitting needle.

But nothing worked – not a bent hairgrip, or a safety pin.

There was a bang from the door of the flat, and thumpy footsteps: Dad.

Billie leaped up, gripping the metal box tight behind her back. Sam slid the open suitcase behind the bed, out of sight.

'Hello, hello – up to mischief, are we?' said Dad, opening the door.

'No!' they both said, at once.

He chuckled. 'Don't worry, I do *not* want to know. Sam, your mums are back, want you to head home with them. Time to say goodbye, angel.'

'See you at school,' said Sam, turning to cross her fingers secretly as she left. *Good luck*, it meant.

Billie crossed hers too. 'See you at school.'

The moment they were gone, she slid the zipped-up suitcase properly under her bed, and the locked box under her pillow, safe.

Then she sat staring at her project cover, beaming.

All she had to do now was find the key, and she could unlock Mum completely.

Hi Mum,

I've been thinking about things you might lock in that box.

So far I have:

- half a bar of gold (so it fits)
- a big key to another box with a whole bar of gold in it
- a secret gold medal you won doing secret athletics or something
- diamonds
- a digital camera with a secret message on it that you filmed just for me
- surprising documents that reveal you are actually the Queen of a small European nation – which means I'm a princess (the documents are in a waterproof box sealed with a waxy blob, which is why it rattles instead of just sounding papery) – which you nobly walked away from to get married but now need me to come and rule instead of doing homework about parabolas
- something I haven't thought of yet but is even better than any of those.

It's exciting having a mystery to solve. If you felt like leaving me a sign about where the key is, that would be even more exciting. If you've lost it, then maybe you could direct me to some dynamite. (That was Sam's idea. It'll have to be very careful dynamite that doesn't blow up gold/cameras/secret documents, but they probably have that in Heaven, so send me some of that.)

This is going to make you so much more heroic than Jessica Ennis-Hill, I can tell.

Lots of love,
Amen,
Bye

CHAPTER 15

Billie spent the next week trying, and failing, to open the box with a series of small wiry poking objects.

This was the trouble with being a real person, not one in a film: locks were very good at staying locked.

On Friday she left the box under her pillow when she came home from school. She did all her homework straight away. Then she changed into jeans and a red-and-yellow stripy top, tied her hair up in a fluffy ponytail, and went down to get the flat ready for Efe's practice sleepover.

She found Raffy – in pyjama bottoms and socks – and Michael, still in his school uniform – playing something called Wartime Deathball in the living room. Raffy was hiding behind the armchair, scrumpling up balls of newspaper and firing them across the room at Michael, who was crouched behind the kitchenette counter, ducking and trying to hit them back with a frying pan. There was paper everywhere: piled up on the back of the sofa, and all over the carpet.

'Oi! No!' shouted Billie, marching between them and throwing out her arms.

A ball bounced off her ear.

'Sorry,' mumbled Raffy, just the top of his head poking out from the armchair. 'That wasn't meant to hit you.'

Billie sighed, picked up the bin and began to scoop paper balls into it, along with a bigger one that was brown and shiny, and turned out to be made of parcel tape all wound together around more paper.

'Nooo!' wailed Raffy, launching himself across the room at her, and wrestling the sticky ball out of her hands. 'Not Mr Pantalon!' He hugged the ball to his chest, cooing at it softly.

'Why is it called Mr Pantalon?' asked Billie warily, not entirely sure she wanted to know.

"Cos he lost his trousers,' said Raffy, as if this was obvious. 'That's, like, his life quest. To find them.'

'And 'cos he's French,' added Michael, joining them. 'See?' He turned the ball of tape so that she could see it wore a Post-it note with a moustache drawn on it.

'OK,' said Billie, backing away. 'I'm very sorry for trying to throw away Mr Pantalon. Maybe you should put him in your bedroom so he's safe.'

'There are trousers in there,' said Michael slowly.

'Come on, Mr Pantalon,' said Raffy, tucking the ball under his arm. 'I'm feeling lucky.'

'Oi! Come back and tidy!'

They kept walking.

'Gabriel would help me tidy up . . .'

'Nah, he wouldn't, though,' said Michael.

'Who d'you think invented Wartime Death-ball?' said Raffy.

Billie glared. 'He would if I went and got Dad and Dad told him to . . .'

By the time Efe arrived, the flat was spotless, and the boys were sitting on the sofa very meekly, with the PlayStation's sound turned down low.

Her Auntie Esther brought her in: a roundish

woman with her hair wrapped up in a brightly patterned gele, thick glasses and an air of suspicion.

'You did not tell me there would be boys,' she said, glaring at Efe.

Efe was creeping backwards, her chin tucked in, looking as if she hadn't thought there would be boys either.

'It's just my brothers,' said Billie quickly.

'They very rude boys,' said Auntie Esther, glaring at Billie now. 'They don't stand up, say hello when an auntie come by?'

'Hiya!' called Raffy, waving from the sofa.

'Hello,' said Michael, a bit more politely now that Billie was glaring at him. 'Um. Good afternoon. Welcome to our home.'

Raffy snorted.

'They're nice boys really,' said Billie. 'Raffy'll be at work later tonight, so he won't even be here. And Michael is . . . basically a Labrador.'

'Hey!'

'Bruv,' said Raffy, elbowing him, eyes still on the TV. 'I just totally stole all your gold and your followers and you just let me. You are well Labrador.'

137

Auntie Esther pushed her lips out, Efe looked like she might climb under her skirt to hide – and then the front door banged and Dad Splendide appeared, all smiles and handshakes and shooing the boys up so that the auntie could have the good armchair, and that fixed everything.

Sam arrived at half past six on her bike, clutching a pillow printed with the Brazilian flag under one arm, with a tray of oaty flapjacks balanced on the handlebars.

'Don't get too hopeful – it's got grated carrots in,' she said with a sigh.

After Auntie Esther had gone, they had tea: pizza again. Then they went up to Billie's bedroom to change into their night things so it would feel more sleepoverish. (They all agreed to turn round and shut their eyes till it was done, so no one would accidentally see anyone's bottom.)

Billie had red pyjamas with rockets on.

Efe had a yellow nightie.

Sam had shorts and a faded yellow T-shirt with PAGET-SKIDELSKY printed across the back in green, with a number 7 underneath.

'I wonder what Ruby's pyjamas are like,' said Efe thoughtfully.

'Too tight,' said Sam, her eyes lighting up. 'Or – pink with little kittens on.'

'Do you think we should've invited her too?' said Efe.

There was an uncomfortable pause.

Billie shook her head. 'She said she didn't need any sleepover practice. Anyway, she lives miles away.'

Willesden wasn't miles, really. Or at all. But the others both nodded their agreement, so it was all actually right and fair and not mean, definitely.

'So . . . what are the things that happen at a sleepover?' asked Efe.

'Staying up all night whispering instead of going to sleep,' said Sam.

'And nail-painting,' said Billie, remembering Mia's ninth birthday party; hers had stayed sticky for much longer than she'd expected, and stuck her unexpectedly to the carpet. 'Only I haven't got any nail paints, so we'd have to do it with gel pens.'

They did, in rainbows.

They made up dances to all the songs on Billie's phone, and practised them in front of her mirror.

They had a handstand competition.

At half past nine Dad made them hot cocoa with milk, and toast cut into triangles for a snack.

Then they gathered a pile of pillows, cushions and sleeping bags together and made a nest on the floor for Sam. Billie and Efe were supposed to sleep in the beds, but it looked too comfy down there, so they pulled all the bedding off too and put it alongside.

Efe wrapped her hair in a satin cap, ready for bed, and Billie touched her own hair self-consciously. Zahra had never told her to do that, or Mum's little book. But Efe shook her head.

'You don't need to,' she said. 'You have good hair.'

Billie reckened she did, actually and felt better.

'Is it going OK so far?' she asked, turning off all the lights. 'Do you feel better about sleepovers now?'

'My tummy hurts,' said Efe, frowning as she lay down. 'But if it'll be like this at the museum, I might like it.'

'It'll be just like this,' said Sam confidently. 'Only with a big massive dead dinosaur looming over your head.'

Efe sat back up, and Billie had to put all the lights back on.

'Sorry,' said Sam.

They played card games for a bit: Snap, and Cheat. Then Sam picked up a folded scrap of paper that was lying beside Efe's bag. It was torn down one side, and covered in Efe's tiny neat handwriting.

My List of Goals for Life by Efe
1. *Never get divorced*
2. *Kiss Edmond Hudson*
3. *Get ears pierced – age 13*
4. *Get twelve A* in my GCSEs – age 16*
5. *Go to Edinburgh University to study Medicine – age 18*
6. *Discover the cure for cancer – by age 30*
7. *Buy a tropical island*
8. *Learn to fly a plane*
9. *Own a dog*
10. *Go on the Smiler at Alton Towers*

Efe squeaked, and buried her head under a pillow.

'Wow,' said Sam. 'Those are pretty specific. Though I can feel you kind of running out of ambition towards the end there.'

'I really wanted to get to ten,' said Efe, peeping out.

'You can do never getting divorced by just never getting married, so that's easy,' said Billie. 'Edmond Hudson, though?'

Efe smiled shyly. 'He's got pillowy lips.'

Billie had never checked, but she supposed it was possible. 'Let's all write one,' she said.

Sam's list was very short.

1. Be interesting

Billie thought one wasn't enough, but ten was too many.

My Life List of what I want out of life by Billie
1. To be a good bridesmaid
2. To find out if I like kissing
3. To make my mum proud of me

'Doesn't everyone like kissing?' asked Efe.

Billie shrugged. 'I don't know. Don't worry, you can have Edmond Hudson.'

'It's a bit vague,' said Sam. 'Like, not being funny, but how will you know if your mum's proud?'

Billie explained about pigeon poo and signs.

'Well, that's disgusting,' said Sam.

'No, I think it's nice,' said Efe. 'Not the poo part. But that she's watching. I don't think my dad watches over me, and he's only in Germany.'

There was a sharp rap on the bedroom door, and Dad's voice said, '*Some* people got up at half five this morning, Billie, and will be doing that again tomorrow.'

They all lay down in silence, and waited till his footsteps had thumped down, down, down before all sitting up again and giggling.

They sang all the songs from *Frozen*, with new made-up words – until Dad came and opened the door again.

'Go to *sleep*,' he said, this time, sounding cross.

Sam made a small snoring sound, which made Billie giggle, and Dad shut the door with a bang, stomping down the stairs.

143

'Let's just not go to sleep at all,' said Sam, sitting up.

They ate the rest of her flapjacks. Then Sam invented a new game called Sharks! – where the floor was an ocean filled with sharks, and you had to climb around the room without touching the carpet. It was easy enough to jump from the floor-nests to the bed, and then onto the bedside table, and from there you could swing off a hook on the back of the door to reach her desk. But there was a wide gap from the desk chair to the big wardrobe door. Billie managed to loop the belt of her fluffy peach dressing gown round the handle and swing it open, so there was something to hang onto, but it was still a big jump.

'If you fall in, you probably only get, like, one leg at a time chewed off by the sharks, so you can keep going,' said Sam cheerfully.

Efe hesitated on the edge of the chair, then, with a deep breath, launched herself forward. Her arms stretched out hopefully. She seemed to hang in the air for a moment. But instead of grabbing the wardrobe door, she hit it face on. It banged shut. She fell with a thump onto her back, and lay there, quite still.

CHAPTER
16

'Efe!' yelped Billie, jumping down off the desk and kneeling beside her.

'Sharks,' hissed Sam, tiptoeing after her.

Efe opened her eyes. 'Ow,' she said, rubbing her nose.

'Does it hurt? Did you break anything?' said Billie, holding her hand. Michael hurt himself sometimes, at rugby. You had to let him stay still, not move him, and usually fetch him an ice pack. There were two in the freezer, ready.

But Efe stood up by herself, wiggling her fingers and toes to make sure they all still worked.

'Bad wardrobe,' she said, kicking it crossly.

'Yeah, you tell it. You're sure you're OK?

Efe nodded.

But Sam gasped, her face turning pale. 'No, Efe, you're not. Look.'

She pointed to the back of Efe's yellow nightie, and a bright splotch of red by her bottom.

Efe craned round, trying to see. Then she gasped too. 'Am I hurt?' she whispered. 'Am I *dying*?' She patted herself all over. 'Nothing is broken. Nothing is broken!'

'Er,' said Sam, looking at Billie. 'Do you think . . . ?'

'Ohhh,' said Billie. Then she smiled, relief swishing through her insides. 'It's OK, Efe! You're not dying and you're not broken. It's your period.'

Efe looked at them both darkly.

'It's, um, just a thing girls' bodies do. Did no one tell you?'

Efe thought hard. 'My mum told me something about bees one time. And I found a book in my room about sperms. And also bees again. But . . . not this.'

'Sorry.'

'So – this happened to you too?' whispered Efe, hopeful.

'Not yet,' said Billie.

Sam shook her head too.

Billie gave Efe's arm a squeeze. 'It's OK, I

know what to do. You just need some pad things to go in your knickers.'

Except she didn't have any, not yet.

And it was now after midnight.

'I feel squidgy,' moaned Efe, wrapping her arms round herself. 'I don't like it. Make it go away.'

'It's OK,' said Billie firmly. She would make it OK.

'Is there a special secret emergency period-things delivery service we could phone up?' asked Sam. 'Like ordering a curry?'

Billie didn't think there was.

'I could ride my bike down to my house and ask my mums for some . . .'

Efe looked appalled.

'They might be a bit cross about being woken up, though.'

Billie frowned. Dad would be too, especially since he was already cross.

Raffy was at work, emptying the bins in some fancy office block somewhere in the city.

'Stay here,' said Billie. 'I know what to do.'

She darted downstairs.

Fifteen minutes later, Michael appeared in the hallway, his coat damp from the rain, and handed her a plastic bag. 'I got a few different ones, 'cos there were loads and it was confusing. And I got chocolate as well. When Natasha gets hers, she always wants to eat chocolate.'

Billie thought she could see, nearly, why all those girls wanted to put their lips on his face. She gave him a tight hug, and hurried back up to her room.

Efe was now wrapped in Billie's peachy dressing gown. She pulled the hood tight around her head with a squeak. 'You told your *brother*? But . . . he's a *boy*.'

'It's fine! Boys know about periods too – they're not a secret.'

Raffy and Michael did, anyway. She remembered Dad sitting the three of them down together, and explaining it. She'd cried when she found out it would only happen to her, not them. And Raffy had tried to leave. But Dad had said that Raffy and Michael – and Gabriel, and all other boys – would spend lots of their lives being friends with people who had periods, and working with them, and maybe one day they'd live with one and be in love with them, so they ought to know all about them too.

'My mums told us when we were five,' said Sam. 'At school the next day I put raspberry jam on Sam's trousers and told everyone it proved he was actually a girl too. He didn't think it was very funny. Neither did the teachers. And no one else's mums had told them, so everyone thought it meant if you sat on a jam sandwich, it turned you into a girl. Packed lunches went a bit scary for a while. In the end they banned jam. They said it was because of the pips – but it was me really.' She smiled with remembered pride.

Billie fetched a bundle of clean clothes from her drawer. Then she took Efe to the bathroom and showed her the instructions on the packet of pads: how to peel off the backing and stick them on her knickers.

'I'll do that bit by myself,' whispered Efe, from underneath the dressing-gown hood.

Billie agreed that was best.

She waited outside while Efe had a wash and changed her clothes.

They tiptoed back upstairs and lay down in their nests, Efe nibbling on her chocolate bar.

'I am totally making Sam bring me chocolate when it happens to me,' said Sam.

Efe rolled over with a sigh. 'I wish I had brothers,' she said.

CHAPTER
17

The next morning Efe crossed off *Edmond Hudson* on her Life List and put *Kiss Michael Bright* instead.

'You don't mind, do you?'

Billie didn't. She was pretty sure Efe would never put her tongue in Michael's mouth without even asking.

When Billie and Michael arrived at the school gates on Monday morning, she was waiting there, with a huge smile and a sugary doughnut in a paper bag.

'Hi, Michael Bright,' she said, handing him the bag.

'Hi, Efe,' he said back, smiling shyly, before being pulled away into a crowd of Year 10 girls. 'Thank you!'

Efe glowed.

Sam skidded up on her bike. 'Hey. How's

your . . . ?' She made a vague circle motion towards her insides. 'Is it still happening?'

Efe screwed up her face unhappily. 'Yes. I thought it would be over right away, but it just carries on and on. It's very terrible.'

Billie didn't like to be the one to tell her it would happen again next month, and the one after – but it seemed Efe was now very well-informed. Her mum had bought a cake, and all her aunties had come round to celebrate her *womanliness*.

'What are you all whispering about?' said Ruby, appearing beside Billie.

Efe gave a tiny shake of her head: *Nope*.

'Um. Nothing,' said Sam quickly. 'Just a joke from the sleepover – you wouldn't understand.'

'Oh. I see,' said Ruby in a small voice.

'It wasn't a funny joke,' murmured Billie.

But Ruby flicked back her hair, looking away. 'It's fine. I was *so* busy all weekend shopping with my dad. My real dad, not my stepdad. He misses me awfully, so he always buys me a *lot* of presents and takes me to McDonald's *whenever* I want.'

No one really knew what to say to that.

'Actually, one of the presents he bought me is

for the *real* sleepover at half-term,' she said. 'It's very secret. I'll have to sneak it in, or we might get into awful trouble. And I'll have to give you all very secret instructions for what to do, because each of you will need to bring a Required Offering to be allowed to join in. Unless . . . you are all coming to the *real* sleepover, aren't you?'

They all nodded.

Ruby's chin lifted, and she smiled sweetly at Billie. 'Oh, good. Because it would be such a shame if anyone got left out.'

She spun on her heel, and began to march across the yard. Then she turned. 'Oh! And here are some of my spare Hero project notes, Efe,' she said, reaching into her bag and producing a red plastic folder stuffed with typed pages. 'I wasn't sure you'd have time to work on it this weekend, because of having to practise being asleep, whereas I'm very efficient at organizing my time, and also highly motivated.'

It was interesting, Billie thought, how Ruby could make even doing a nice, kind thing sound annoying.

'Thanks,' whispered Efe, looking at the ground.

Miss Eagle had asked them all to bring in their Hero projects so far, so she could check that they were working hard. Today she was wearing a lemon-coloured dress with tiny rainbow dots, and a miniature fan-shaped clip in her pinned-up hair.

'You look like an ice cream, miss,' said Big Mohammad.

'Thank you, Mohammad.'

Ruby's project had thirty-eight laminated pages, filled with closely typed information and printed colour photographs. Miss Eagle looked like she might fall over just trying to pick it up.

'I haven't even got to the 2012 Olympics yet, miss,' said Ruby, beaming. 'Jessica Ennis-Hill's just *so* interesting, and there are *so* many Greatest Achievements to put in. My stepdad's put together a nutrition regime to match hers too – he works for NutriGenix, you know; they work with all the best athletes – so the sports complex will be able to benefit from my project for ever.'

'Oh!' said Miss Eagle.

'He hasn't had time to write it down for me quite yet,' said Ruby, her voice going quiet. 'But he will. There's lots of time left.'

'All very impressive, Ruby,' said Miss Eagle, handing it back. 'Well done. Billie?'

Billie felt quite hot around her neck as she took her project out and laid it on the desk. There was still only a cover, and lots of blank pages with headings written on: 'Early Life' and 'Surprising Facts'.

Miss Eagle flipped through the empty pages doubtfully. 'You have a lot of work to do here. You're not finding it too tricky, are you? Not too . . . emotional?'

Billie could feel Ruby's beady eyes, greedily watching.

The hot feeling around her neck got hotter.

'Nah, miss,' she said quickly. 'I'm, um, still compiling my research data. It's going to be brilliant. I just want to make her proud, miss.'

Miss Eagle smoothed her hand over the angel image on the cover before handing it back with a kind sigh. 'I'm sure she would be, lovely.' Then she went off to explain to Halid that, no, some boxing gloves and a Chicken Cottage menu did not count as an English project.

'Hmm,' said Ruby, flipping through the empty

155

pages too, as if to check there wasn't a secret brilliant laminated project hidden inside.

'What?' said Billie.

Ruby slapped the cover closed. 'Oh, nothing,' she said airily. 'Nothing at all.'

After Miss Eagle had checked all the projects, she clapped her hands together. 'Now, who here has heard of *Hercules*?'

Billie put her hand up, then hesitated, in case she didn't mean the Disney one. But she did, except he was also from Roman times and Greek times (but called Herakles), and in lots of different versions.

Miss Eagle turned on the projector and played the start of an old TV show to prove it.

The Hercules man in it was enormous, with giant muscly arms like a toy. Apparently he had 'Legendary Journeys'. Most of them seemed to involve him taking his top off before punching a big snake.

Billie wasn't keen. She didn't like his face. He was sort of leathery, and glistening.

But Madison wolf-whistled from the back of the class, and Lianne shouted, 'You allowed to show us this, like, sexy stuff, miss?'

Most of the class were watching with their mouths slightly open.

Then there was a gentle tap on the door, and Michael walked in, fresh from PE, in his rugby shorts and a tight shirt, to give Miss Eagle a message about excess noise from the building site – and suddenly all eyes that had been glued to the glisteny man zoomed in on him.

'Hey, Michael Bright,' cooed Acacia.

Madison began drumming on the table.

Miss Eagle hopped up, flushing as she paused the video on an especially rippling bit of torso. 'Yes, well, that's enough of that, thank you,' she said, shooing Michael back out as the drumming grew louder.

He threw Billie a vague look of terror before he fled, to a chorus of, 'Bye, Michael Bright,' and 'Come back soon, Michael Bright.'

Billie felt her cheeks grow hot.

Miss Eagle switched off the video, tugging her cardigan into place and smoothing her hair. 'Settle down, please.'

'That was dead good, miss,' shouted Madison.

'He can be my hero anytime,' said Lianne, and

she did a sort of grindy dance against the desk until Madison pinged a pencil at her head.

Billie wasn't sure if she meant Hercules or Michael, and decided she didn't want to know. Either way, it was pretty clear that everyone else liked the glisteny man – until Miss Eagle told them that Hercules killed his wife and his six sons, at which point they all went off him a bit.

'He *had* been driven insane by the goddess Hera at the time,' said Edmond Hudson, in his high, polite voice. 'And he performed the Twelve Labours of Hercules to say sorry.'

'Very good, Edmond,' said Miss Eagle.

'Ten points to Gryffindor,' shouted Alfie.

Then the bell rang for the end of the lesson, and everyone looked quite relieved.

Hi Mum,

I have been thinking a lot about kissing today.

Don't worry, I haven't suddenly gone all pervy like the Year 9 boys who flick up all the girls' skirts when we're waiting outside ICT. They did it again today, and we all saw Acacia's pants. Big white ones. I held my arms down over my skirt, so even if they did flip mine, all they'd get is a bit of knee. But from now I'm going to wear my best pants on ICT days, just in case.

Anyway, I have tried imagining kissing Hercules, for science and for my Life List, but that leathery one from Miss Eagle's video looks slippery – like you might slide right off his face.

I don't want to kiss Edmond Hudson, even if he has got pillowy lips.

I thought about kissing Miss Eagle at the school sleepover, standing on tiptoes while Big Mohammad says, 'You look like a lesbian, miss' – but she doesn't, really. Sam says you can't tell by looking, but I'm pretty sure. Anyway, I think I just like her dresses and her shoes, and her being my English teacher.

I don't think there's a single mouth in the whole world I want to put my tongue in. I hope that doesn't make me weird.

Did you know about the Twelve Labours of Hercules? They were all quite stabby. I can see why Disney skipped a few and put in some jokes instead. Anyway, I've decided that's the main difference between Year 6 and Year 7. Goodbye, cartoons. Hello, tops off and stabbing and everyone talking about Michael's thighs: 12 – not even a 12A. And I'm only eleven, which is actually quite difficult, actually. It's like you aren't little and cute any more, and you aren't a confident sexy teen with candyfloss hair and big hoops either. You are just a nothing waiting to be something, except I am already a lot of somethings.

I like the somethings I am. I don't want any new ones.

Lots of love,
Amen,
Bye

CHAPTER
18

On the bus home Billie sat deep in thought – so much so that she hardly noticed Michael was sitting by himself in the seat in front.

'Coach Jen says I need to stay focused, yeah? So I told all the girls they have to stop kissing me because I've got tryouts coming up,' he said proudly when they got to their stop.

'You do know you could just tell them to stop kissing you anyway?' said Billie.

Michael nodded slowly, like he didn't really believe her.

At home, she walked up the narrow steps to her bedroom and changed out of her school uniform. She put her empty, just-a-cover project on her little desk and stared at all the blank pages. She slid the metal box from under her pillow, and rattled it thoughtfully.

It would all, definitely, be fine, because she

was Team Bright and Team Bright always was. And it was, still, totally actually exciting to not really know anything about Mum. But Miss Eagle's words kept whispering round and round in her head – *Too tricky? Too emotional?* – and a small peely corner of herself felt a tiny bit not happy, like a sticker that was stuck on not quite straight.

She knelt on the worn carpet and peered under her bed. She pushed Raffy's old kite (broken, but he wouldn't throw it away) aside, and a tub of Lego, and pulled out a long white box. Resting on top were all Gabriel's old GCSE Art sketchbooks. She picked up the top one, blowing dust off the cover. Inside, the pages were crammed with drawings of Highgate Cemetery – solemn angel statues wound about the ankles with ivy; bigger coffin-like tombs with carvings on the side; twisted old trees – all in the same style as his drawing of Mum: charcoals and chalks, smooth bold strokes and fingerprint smudges.

She turned to the best page, the one she knew was Gabriel's favourite: an angel, head bowed, hands clasped around a drooping bundle of flowers, eyes closed as if it was pretending to be somewhere more cheerful. Pieces of it filled up every other space on the page, wasting no space, in close up, the wings or the curve of the lips sketched in loving detail. She touched the wings. (You weren't supposed to. Charcoal rubbed off, even if you sprayed it with hairspray. But she did it anyway.)

She was still a bit cross that Mum's grave was just a stone with her name on when you could have an epic big angel with massive wings. The funeral had been very disappointing. (You weren't supposed to think that either, but sometimes brains do what they want.)

She put the sketchbooks carefully aside, and pulled the white box close.

MUMMY ♥ BILLIE, it said, in glittery pink letters, glued on not quite straight. Her Memory Box; made so she wouldn't forget, as if mums were people you might.

Billie shut her eyes as tightly as she could, and thought very religious and prayerful good thoughts with her hands pressed reverently together.

Then she took a deep breath, lifted the lid, and took all the things out, laying them around her like a fan.

A paper doll, hand drawn, with one leg too

long, and all the clothes they'd made for her: pyjamas with orange and purple stripes; a clown outfit; a party dress.

A kiss, in pinky lipstick, on a card with a poem on it about remembering and far-off lands.

A hand-made book of haircare: photographs and tips snipped from magazines, *For my beautiful girl as she grows.*

A list of questions and answers, written out in a grown-up's hand:

Will Father Christmas still come?
When will you come back?
Can I still go to Sasha's birthday party at Mr Doodle's Fun Hutch?

A letter, soft around the edges from being held.

It hadn't worked. She'd hoped there might be something new – a clue, a hint, a secret special something that she'd never understood, and that, now she was so extremely old and grown up and Year 7ish, might magically reveal itself. With special effects. Or a genie. Perhaps even a tiny key that would fit into a tiny lock.

But it was the same as always. Just memories, not Mum. All beloved and familiar. All totally useless for a Hero project.

She went downstairs and got an orange squash and two biscuits. She ate them staring at Mum's photo in the alcove, still thinking all her most good and worthy thoughts, until she heard footsteps, then the front door banging shut. Michael, going out for a run.

Then she tiptoed over and stood outside Raffy and Michael's bedroom door.

Raffy would be out, on another trial day at another new job: this time selling mobile phones in a shop in Kilburn.

She wasn't exactly allowed in when they weren't there.

But it had been her room once; hers and Michael's. And it was for school, and to beat Ruby, and for her mum, which were all good reasons that made it definitely OK, actually.

She pushed the door open and clicked it shut behind her quickly.

Michael's bed was neatly made, with a row of small gold cups and trophies on the shelf above.

Raffy's side was like a tidal wave of undone laundry threatening to wash them all away, overflowing from open drawers onto crumby old plates, his bed a mound of pillows and duvet all piled in a heap.

Billie kneeled down and peered in Michael's bottom drawer, looking for his Memory Box. It had stickers of runners all over the sides – he was going to be a runner back then, before he suddenly sprouted upwards and outwards and got slower, but strong – and inside was more of the same: photographs and letters, a clay tile with fingerprints pressed into it, a cinema ticket.

There was no secret surprise. Nothing you could use in a project.

She put it all back and slid it into the drawer again.

Wrinkling her nose, she hopped over the piles of stinky jeans and inside-out shirts on Raffy's side. She peered warily into his wardrobe. Inside there were jumbly piles of more clothes, crooked stacks of old PS games, a guitar from that time he was going to learn to play guitar. She shifted a bundle of clothes to one side, and found it: a black cardboard shoebox with *Raphael* written on the side on a simple sticky white label.

When she picked it up, there was a brochure lying on top – a small booklet with a photo of three smiley young people in a park, with *North London Institute of Further Education* stamped across the top.

The booklet fell open at one well-thumbed page.

Course: NVQ1 Hospitality and Catering –
Enfield Campus
An introductory course for trainee chefs, kitchen assistants, wait staff, front of house, receptionists and other hotel staff, leading to a Certificate in Hospitality.

With a little gasp, Billie sat down on the bundled-up duvet on the bed behind her.

'Aaaargh!' wailed the bed, and suddenly the mound of pillows and duvet reared into life as Raffy leaped up from underneath the covers.

'Aaaargh!' yelled Billie, falling backwards into the wardrobe, sending the guitar and the *Raphael* box toppling to the floor with a crash and a twang.

167

'What're you waking me up for?' Raffy growled, rubbing his eyes and wrapping the duvet round him. (He was only wearing pants and socks.)

'Why are you here and not at work?' Billie shouted back, clambering awkwardly out of the wardrobe and rubbing her elbow where she'd bumped it.

Raffy looked sheepish, and pulled the duvet tighter. 'It wasn't my fault! I sort of told an old lady she didn't need a smartphone on a forty-quid-a-month contract, because she didn't. And then I used my staff discount to help a kid buy some headphones 'cos he didn't have enough. And then I got really into this level on *Candy Crush* in the staff room and took, like, an hour's break instead of twenty minutes. So the guy said me working there wasn't going to work out.'

'But that's OK! Because now you can do this instead!' Billie thrust the brochure towards him happily.

Raffy's eyes narrowed, and he snatched it out of her hand. 'You read this?'

'Yes! It's perfect. Clever you! Yay Team Bright!'

Raffy fell back onto the bed, pulling the duvet over his head and groaning.

'Not yay Team Bright?' Billie said. 'Raff?' She prodded his ankle where it stuck out from the duvet until he sat up again.

'It was Gabriel's idea. So I could help Dad out, and he wouldn't be so tired all the time – he could have days off, and watch Mikey's matches, and take you out to movies, and just be, like, a person. And I want all that. But I went to this open day tryout thing and . . . it all just looked like school.'

'Was it going to make you into a husk of a person?'

Raffy's shoulders slumped. 'I'm just no good at that stuff, Bills.' He took the brochure off her with a sad look. 'Don't tell anyone, yeah?'

Billie nodded, feeling very old and grown up. 'I won't. Our secret.'

Raffy chucked the brochure vaguely in the direction of the wardrobe, and smiled. 'Anyway, it doesn't matter. I got chatting to that old lady with the smartphone – they get lonely, you know – and she was telling me there's this new party shop opening right by her. You get to dress up in all the costumes and wigs and stuff, to, like, advertise it. I can do that. So I'm going down there tomorrow, see if they need people.'

'Is that what you really want to do, Raff? Work in a party shop? For ever?'

He shrugged. 'It's what I want to do this week. For ever's ages, Bills.'

That was true. Billie wanted to be a doctor, or a paramedic, or Pocahontas. But she wasn't sure she'd want to be them always.

'OK, then. Good luck.'

'Thanks, Bills.' He snuggled back down in the bed, then sat up. 'Hey – what were you doing in here?'

'Oh. Um. I was looking for your Memory Box, to help with my Hero project, because it might be heroic, maybe. I would've asked if I'd known you were here!' she added quickly. 'It's for school!'

Raffy climbed out of bed, kicking clothes aside, and picked up the *Raphael* box. He gripped it tightly, his face closing over.

'Some things are private,' he said softly. 'Some things you don't go nosing about in. Not for

170

school, or any reason. You hear me? I mean it, Bills. Pick something else for your project.'

And he slammed the box back into the wardrobe and pushed the door shut. Then he got back into bed, pulled the duvet up and turned his back.

Hi Mum,
     Please watch over Raffy loads and loads?
     And me as well, because being old continues to
be actually very confusing.

     Lots of love,
     Amen,
     Bye

CHAPTER
19

Billie spent the rest of the week feeling quite fuzzy-brained.

'How's your project going?' Ruby would ask every morning. (She had taken to carrying hers around in a huge folder tied with black ribbons, poking out of a NutriGenix sports bag.)

'Fine,' Billie would say.

'You want to ask any more questions about your mama, bright girl?' asked Dad when they cooked pasta bake together on Thursday night.

'No thanks,' said Billie, feeling Raffy's eyes on her back, watchful (which was quite alarming, since he'd spent the day dressed as a vampire at the costume shop and still had blood dribbles round his mouth).

The locked box stayed under her pillow, and the pages of her Hero project remained empty, untouched.

And no pigeon poos came along to tell her what to do now. (She spent a lot of time standing under railings, or trees, or the ledgy bits outside church, to give them all their very best chance.)

The next Saturday she slowly did her jobs of laundry and tidying her room, then went down to the café for her bacon bap.

The Paget-Skidelskys were already leaving their now-traditional table, cheerfully arguing about superheroes ('They're just pants! They don't give you magic powers if you wear them over your trousers!'), and invited her to come home with them, as usual.

Billie hesitated, remembering what Raffy had said about Dad having time to be a person. There were piles of cups waiting to be rinsed and put through the big dishwasher, and a queue of people waiting.

'I could stay and help,' she whispered, slipping behind the counter.

But Dad shushed her at once, shooing her out. 'Hey, you know you're not allowed back here. You go and have fun for me, angel. Now, who's next?'

The Paget-Skidelskys' kitchen table was covered in Hero project pages: a confusing mixture of Brazilian footballers and superheroic comic strips. Neither of the Sams had bothered with laminating the pages, or tying them in a fancy ribboned folder – but it was still quite disheartening.

'Ugh, projects,' said Dr Skidelsky, scavenging for her coffee cup under all the pages. 'Does your kitchen table look like this, Billie?'

Billie's flat didn't have a kitchen table, and even if it did . . .

She sat on a chair, feeling very gloomy. 'Not really. I *have* started. And I really love the cover I've made. But now my brother says I shouldn't be doing a project about Mum at all. So I think maybe I might change it to be about Jessica Ennis-Hill instead.'

'You can't!' said Sam hotly. 'Then all three of you will be doing that and *I'll* be the left-out one.'

Dr Paget frowned at her, as if filing away a conversation for later. Then she turned and looked at Billie seriously. 'That seems like quite a big decision for something so personal. Why do you think he asked you to change it?'

Billie shrugged, tucking her knees up and wrapping her arms round them as Surprise came snuffling under her chair. 'Don't know. No one else minds. Dad said it was sweet. Michael said she would've liked it. Gabriel too. It's only Raffy.'

She squeaked as Surprise jumped right up and rested on her elbow with his soft-padded paws. Billie could feel his hot doggy breath, ever so close.

'Argh! Ridiculous dog – don't chew people who don't like being chewed,' said Dr Skidelsky, pushing him away.

Billie stayed all scrunched up in her chair until Dr Paget leaned in close.

'Billie, why don't you and me go for a little grown-up chat somewhere a bit quieter, away from silly dogs and all the rest? Would you like that?'

Sam rolled her eyes and groaned – but Billie thought she would, actually, absolutely like a little grown-up chat.

She followed Dr Paget down the wood-floored hall and into their front room. There was no TV, or PlayStation, or kitchen smell. There were two plush golden sofas facing one another across a low table, and lots of books on shelves.

'Is this where you do the therapy stuff with all your sad families?'

Dr Paget smiled. 'That's right.' She sat down, and nodded for Billie to sit on the other sofa.

She did, and felt very grown-up indeed.

'I wonder – would you like to tell me what happened to your mum? How she died? You don't have to.'

'No, it's OK, I like talking about her,' said Billie. And she told the familiar version she'd heard Dad tell so many times: how she'd got ill not long after Gabriel was born, really ill, hospital ill – and then she got better so she had Raffy and Michael and Billie, and then one day she went into the doctor's with a cold she couldn't quite kick and came out with terminal cancer.

'They said she had three months to live, but it was a bit less than two really. She didn't have all the chemotherapy stuff where your hair falls out, or any of that. She just got really tired. And then, for the last few days, she was in a hospice and she was mostly asleep. I know it doesn't sound very heroic. She did cry. We all cried. But I bet she was brave on the inside. I reckon just dying at all is brave, isn't it?'

Dr Paget smiled. 'Well, I haven't had to find out yet — but I think I know what you mean. It's interesting, how often we use the word *brave* when we talk about cancer, don't you think? I talk to families dealing with terminal illness sometimes, helping them to talk about their feelings and their worries. And they always say *brave*. And *heroic*. It's a lot to ask of someone who's not well.'

'She was, though! I bet she was.'

'I'm sure she tried to be. I think we all would. But she also might have felt angry, or unlucky, or in pain. I wonder if we use *brave* and *heroic* to avoid thinking about that. Billie, how old were you when all this happened?'

'Five. That's why I only remember some stuff.'

Dr Paget raised an eyebrow and looked thoughtful. 'And Raffy?'

Billie counted back on her fingers. 'Eleven, like me.'

'Oh. That's interesting. How do you think you might feel if it happened now? To you now?'

Billie fiddled with her thumbnail. 'It'd be better, because I would have had six more years of having a mum. And six more years of Dad being a bit less tired and always at work. But . . . I might be even more sad, because I'd know what it meant. I didn't understand it, not really. Because mums don't just leave, do they? So . . . I think I thought she was going to come back.'

A tight little ache wrapped itself around her middle, like a belt done up too many notches. Hurrying home to show her mum this very brilliant painting of a giraffe from school. Fighting with Michael over whose turn it was to choose the channel, or tripping and scuffing her knees and calling out 'Mummy!' all cross – and then there'd be a drop in her stomach like she'd fallen off a high brick wall and never hit the ground, kept on falling – as it came back in a rush and knocked her down. Knocked the air right out of her lungs. The worst feeling ever. Forgetting, and having to remember again. So she traced it into the pillow with a fingertip before she went to sleep, wrote it in her notebooks, on the palm of her left hand in purple felt-tip pen: *Mummy is dead.* Till Dad saw it once, written on her skin, his face crumply, and then that was the worst feeling ever too.

It wasn't just sad.

It was guilty, and anxious, and slippery under her feet. A new world with new rules.

You got used to it. But it was in you now, that bad feeling. For ever.

'And how did Raffy feel back then, do you think?' said Dr Paget gently.

'I think he would've known she wasn't going to come back, ever, all along . . .' Billie said slowly. She shifted on her chair unhappily. 'I'm making him sad, aren't I? That's why he wants me to pick something else. I don't want to make him sad.'

Dr Paget smiled. 'I'm sure you don't. But perhaps feeling sad about something sad is worth doing.'

'Like in *The Jungle Book*, when you think Baloo's dead?' said Billie. 'I always cry, even though I know he isn't. And, um . . . I sort of enjoy the crying. That is definitely my favourite bit.'

'There you are. Experiencing our feelings . . . it's an important part of being human. But for some funny reason, we're not very good at letting boys cry. We tell them to be *brave* and *heroic* instead. So an eleven-year-old boy in a big family like yours . . . He might still have a lot of feelings tucked away.'

'And my Hero project could help them come untucked?'

'Maybe. Just don't expect him to say thank you right away. Untucked feelings usually make a bit of a mess, in my experience. You might have to be a bit brave yourself.'

The wooden door banged open.

'Have you finished being nosy and weird yet?' said Sam. 'Because Mum K says we're going to bake muffins, and 'cos you're a guest, if you help, we might get her to put chocolate chips in instead of broad beans.'

'I said blueberries, not broad beans!' yelled a voice from the kitchen. 'For heaven's—'

In the end they made two batches: one blueberry, one chocolate chip.

Billie took one of each home and left them outside Raffy's bedroom door, like a secret way to say *Sorry*, and *Don't be sad*, and *I love you*.

CHAPTER

20

Two weekends later, the little yellow car zoomed up to the peely-paint front door next to The Splendide, and collected Billie for her next round of bridesmaiding.

Dress shopping.

Which turned out not to be at all like the usual shopping at Asda or Next or the Emporium on Kilburn High Road, where Dad or Raffy or Michael or all three would walk behind her, mumbling, till she found something she liked. The shop Alexei had chosen was so fancy you needed to make an appointment to even try things on – and although there were dresses in the window, most of the shop was velvet sofas, changing rooms and empty space.

'You could've warned me,' Billie whispered to Gabriel, shuffling in her trainers and hoodie and fussing with her fluffy ponytail. There were huge gold-framed mirrors everywhere too.

'How often do you think I go bridesmaid's-dress shopping?' he whispered back.

He gave a jolt as a woman wearing a grey buttoned-up waistcoat offered him a peppermint tea and a neck massage. Alexei was chatting away happily to another woman with perfect short grey hair all glued into place, laughing and kissing her on both cheeks.

Billie was given a big pile of catalogues and a pink velvet chair to sit on while she looked.

'What do you think, huh?' said Alexei, leaning over her shoulder. 'Full Disney princess? Bows and frills?'

Billie whispered up. 'There aren't any prices.'

He twinkled. 'You know what they say: if you have to ask, you can't afford.'

Then they wheeled out a rack of things for her to try.

'The scheme is white and gold, yes?' said the grey-haired woman. 'Charming. Perfect for winter. But another accent colour would pop beautifully . . .

a purple, something strong . . . or paler – lilac, maybe, with that skin tone?'

Billie was pressed into a changing room with a selection of purple things.

The waistcoat woman kept peeping round the curtain to offer help, even though Billie had no clothes on and didn't even know her name – but the zips were fiddly, and there were weird under-skirts and linings and tight bits to wiggle your arms into.

She wished she'd worn fancier pants. And a bra that hadn't been through the wash so many times the elastic had gone wiggly.

The first dress was ruffly and tight across her tummy, and Alexei wrinkled his nose at once.

'Too cheap.'

The next one went down to the floor.

'Too old.'

The next she got stuck in, in a forest of net and straps, and she took it off before even bothering to come out of the changing room.

Billie peeked out and pointed at a minty dress on the rack. Tiana from *The Princess and the Frog* wore minty green. She wasn't Billie's favourite, though for birthdays everyone always bought her Tiana stuff from the Disney shop. But the skirt stuck out like Miss Eagle's dresses. It looked pretty.

'White, gold, mint . . . a deep green might be more seasonal . . .' said the grey-haired woman outside doubtfully. 'But we should try the fit, anyway.'

Billie wriggled happily as the waistcoat woman zipped her in. The dress felt soft and satiny. She could imagine herself in little white shoes and white gloves, her hair twisted up in a goddess braid like a halo, and Big Mohammad saying, *You look like a bridesmaid, Billie* . . .

She swept the curtain back.

'Oh dear,' said Alexei.

'Not quite enough up top,' said the waistcoat woman, in a loud whisper.

Even Gabriel shook his head.

Billie looked in the mirror and saw at once that they were right. The dress didn't look at all like it had in her head. The straps were falling off her shoulders, the waist was down round her hips, and the space for her boobies was all baggy.

Billie pulled the curtain tight and put her jeans and hoodie back on as quickly as she could, while Alexei and the grey-haired woman stood outside discussing mint versus emerald, lemon versus gold. There was another catalogue on a little glass dressing table, so she flipped through.

This one *did* have the prices in.

Billie felt sick.

Everything she had tried on cost impossible money. Dresses that cost as much as a car; dresses where there was a comma in the price. Suddenly she was glad that none of them had fitted.

She swished the curtain back, and the waistcoat woman laughed, clapping her hands. 'Oh, pumpkin! We've barely started! There are racks and racks more to try – or you might like to go bespoke . . . you know, have something made; that would do away with any, er, awkward fit issues . . .'

Alexei was led aside to flip through a new set of catalogues. 'Gabriel, come here – your wedding too, right?' he said.

'Right,' Gabriel muttered, hurrying over.

Billie sat in Gabriel's chair, feeling squirmy and not very grown up at all. There was an iPad lying on the arm, in a black leather case with a thick, cream-coloured card tucked inside.

Save the Date!

December 12th

Alexei & Gabriel request your company on their special day

~ venue: to be confirmed ~

R.S.V.P.

December 12th was a Saturday, she knew, because Miss Eagle had told them all their projects needed to be finished on December 11th for the grand unveiling of the new sports centre name.

On the iPad screen was a list of names and addresses, with some names already crossed out.

Federico Cilenti was number seven on the list, with a ? next to his name.

Uncle Fed. The boy with the curtains of hair, pointing up at the CILENTI'S sign. The one who had twirled her.

There was an address underneath.

Billie thought, on reflection, that she could probably forgive a bit of unannounced twirling for the good of her Hero project.

187

Feeling a sudden surge of excitement, she slipped her phone out of her pocket and took a quick photo.

Then she went and tugged on Gabriel's sleeve, pulling him into a corner.

'Can I not try any more dresses on, please? Can I just be a bridesmaid in a normal dress from a normal shop?'

He raised his eyebrows, amused. 'You're the one who's got to wear it, right?'

'Do you think Alexei will mind?'

'He's getting his own way on everything else. Leave it to me.'

Ten minutes later Billie was squeezed into the tiny back seat of Alexei's car, all the way back to Kensal Rise. They didn't talk; just played the radio, extra loud.

Gabriel ran inside, just to say hello, while Alexei let Billie out of the car.

'You sure about this dress, Billie, huh? Maybe we can try another place – you know, we can try on every dress in London . . .'

'I don't want to.'

He laughed. 'You and your brother. You are very alike, you know this? Stubborn.'

Billie hesitated, wondering if a good bridesmaid would say something now about maybe not getting married in an aquarium with horses for two days.

But then Gabriel reappeared, so she let Alexei wrap her up in a hug instead. He fussed with her hoodie for a moment, adjusting the zip.

'You find yourself something pretty, hmm?' he said, kissing her cheek and jumping behind the wheel before Gabriel could get there.

They peeled away with a squeal of tyres.

When Billie put her hand in her hoodie pocket, she felt something bump her fingers.

A tightly furled roll of fifty-pound notes. Ten of them.

Five hundred pounds.

'Crisps,' said Raffy. 'That's what I'd spend it on. Five hundred quid in crisps. I'd, like, empty them all out and jump in. Like a ball pit.'

'You wouldn't.' Michael stared at the money, spread out on his bedspread. 'You'd put it in the bank. Save it up for something big, like new boots.

Or a ticket for the World Cup. Or . . . like, at least you would eat the crisps, not just jump on them.'

Billie glared at both of them. 'Only I can't do any of those, because I'm supposed to buy a *dress*.'

'Yeah, I totally wouldn't do that,' said Raffy, flopping onto his bed.

Billie scooped the notes together, counting them again. They didn't make a big fat stack like in films – but it was still so much.

'Should I give it back? Alexei might be upset, because he's only trying to be nice and I already didn't want his other dresses. Gabriel would want me to give it back. Only Gabriel doesn't know I've got it, so they might argue and have to get their names scraped off their wedding cake so they can sell it to someone else and never get married at all and it'll all be my fault.'

Raffy and Michael both stared at her blankly.

'Ugh,' she said. 'You have no idea how hard bridesmaiding is.'

She stomped up the attic stairs and stuffed the bundle of notes into the holey seam of Zanzibar, her cuddly Tiny Robot Unicorn Friend, stuffing him down the side of her bed for extra secretiveness.

Her hand bumped into the metal box, still under her pillow. She took it out and rattled it. Then sat down at her desk and pulled out a piece of paper.

Dear Uncle Fed,

This is your niece Billie.

I expect I'll see you again quite soon at Gabriel's wedding, but I have to finish my project before then so I am writing to you first.

Since she was your sister, I expect you know a lot of very good facts about my mum — like, did she ever, for example:

— rescue a dog from a fast-moving river?
— perform that hug thing on a person choking on a sweet and save their life?
— run a marathon to raise money for multiple sclerosis and/or other diseases, without mentioning it?
— win a gold medal in the Olympics, very quietly, perhaps in disguise?
— display supernatural powers which she kept secret for years and years to protect her family, e.g. magic ice queen who makes it snow with her fingers, etc.?
— any other surprising heroic behaviour?

Also, do you have any keys — small ones that belonged to my mum? Because technically that means they belong to me and I need them very urgently.

Please reply very quickly. THIS IS FOR SCHOOL.

From Billie

She wrote his address carefully on an envelope, with *URGENT* in red gel pen across the top, added a stamp, and posted it in the letterbox outside.

CHAPTER
21

On the Friday night at the start of half-term, Billie carefully packed her Tiny Robot Unicorn Friends backpack ready for the school sleepover at the museum.

She had her red rocket pyjamas, Gabriel's old sleeping bag, and the strange selection of Required Offerings Ruby had insisted they all bring for her mysterious secret plan: a black jumper, a box of matches, and six maple pecan pastries from the café.

Ruby had refused to give any details; only that they were sworn to secrecy, and that it was going to be the best and most important part of the whole sleepover.

'Nervous?' asked Dad, flipping through her washbag to check for toothpaste.

Billie shook her head. It was exciting, the idea of sleeping in a museum full of dinosaurs – if a bit annoying to not have been the one to think up a mysterious secret plan. But she had been very preoccupied with bridesmaiding, and wondering about kissing, and Raffy, and Mum. Ruby was just picking up the slack and being the interesting friend who thought up dramatic secret things that might get them into trouble, temporarily, until Billie got to be in charge again.

'Have fun,' called Raffy from the sofa. 'Totally don't worry about the ghosts or anything.'

'Ghosts?'

'Yeah. 'Cos, like, everyone knows museums are haunted. All those spooky old cases of stuff . . . all them dead bones . . . I mean, I'm not saying that they all come to life and start eating people at night-time, but . . . WOOOOOOOOO!' He leaped into the hallway, dressed in trailing rags and bandages, his face covered in peeling-off fake green skin and scary white contact lenses that turned his eyes into pinpricks.

'Waaaah!' screamed Billie, slamming back into the wall.

'Eeeeek!' screamed Dad in a squeaky voice, clutching her arm. Then he dropped it very sharply and wagged his finger at Raffy. 'Son, you – you—'

'I'm just getting into character, Dad! There's this band, The Scream? They're doing a Halloween gig and they wanted people to be in the crowd, like, properly dressed up, to freak everyone out. They were going to just hire the costumes, but they liked me being all spooky in the shop, so they hired this with me in it.'

He grinned, all proud – but Dad kept his stern wagging finger up until Raffy's shoulders drooped.

'Sorry, Bills,' he murmured. 'There's no such thing as ghosts, or zombie dinosaurs. Anyway, they wouldn't mess with a load of Year Sevens. Not enough meat on their bones.'

Dad made a low growling noise as Raffy shambled away, grrr-ing and argh-ing. 'Promise me you're going to forget everything he just said and have a brilliant time, angel?'

'Promise,' said Billie. She didn't believe in ghosts.

She went to sit at the top of the flat stairs to wait.

Michael was sitting there too, eating a banana and jiggling one leg.

'You OK?' she said quietly, nudging his shoulder.

It was his U16s trial tomorrow at 9 a.m. Even Raffy thought it was just an ordinary training session – despite Michael getting up even earlier, doing twice as many sit-ups, and eating two peanut-butter sandwiches before each meal all week long.

Michael grinned. 'I'll be good. It's a closed session anyway – you wouldn't be allowed in to cheer me on.'

The doorbell rang: the Paget-Skidelskys, picking Billie up.

'Good luck,' she whispered, crossing her fingers together. Then she rushed back into the kitchenette, gave Dad a quick kiss on the cheek, and sprinted down the stairs.

The Paget-Skidelskys didn't have their own car, so they were going by tube: both Sams, and Dr Paget to make sure they got there.

'Did you bring . . . ?' whispered Sam.

Billie tapped the Required Offerings in the front pocket of her backpack.

'Me too.'

The boy Sam was already in his pyjamas, with trainers and a coat.

'I'm being practical and saving on packing,' he said. 'And I don't want to have to change in front of Seven E.'

Billie didn't either; she couldn't be sure that Acacia would turn round so no one could see anyone's bottom. But she and Sam agreed they would change in the toilets, guarding each other's door in case the locks were wonky.

The walk through the tunnel at South Kensington seemed to go on for ever, with the Sams' wheelie cases sending an eerie rattle echoing off the curving white walls, and lots of teenagers dressed up as zombies and witches heading out to Halloween parties. By the time Dr Paget had ushered them along the queue and into the huge stone doorway of the museum, Billie was feeling quite spooked.

High above, the looming empty eye sockets of Dippy the dinosaur didn't exactly help.

Neither did the spooky cobweb decorations hanging from the walls, or the dimmed lighting, or Big Mohammad and Halid running around in bat costumes shouting, 'Whooooooaaaaah!'

They found Efe curled in a ball under her sleeping bag, quivering.

They all snuggled under it, waiting.

It was strange, seeing everyone in their home clothes. Lianne had black eyeliner coming out of her eyes in big swoops, and a strappy top and flip-flops – even though it was October and freezing. Edmond Hudson was wearing a bow tie and a woolly jumper. Miss Eagle was in proper pyjamas – the stripy sort with a collar – and her hair was tied in two sweet messy bunches. Meanwhile Mr Miller was dressed in a bright orange pumpkin onesie, and looked really quite unhappy about it.

By the time Ruby arrived they'd already handed out snacks and a Dino Trail activity for later. She was wearing a fluffy pale blue jacket, like a muppet with buttons, and carrying something enormous and square under her arm, wrapped in a blanket.

'You'll find out later,' she said, a little smile tugging at her mouth, when asked what was inside. 'At midnight. The *witching hour.*'

'I bet it's a crossbow,' Sam muttered when Ruby went to claim her spot on the floor. 'I've worked it out. This is all some creepy social experiment. They're going to lock the doors and come back in the morning to see which one of us is still alive. You know, like *The Hunger Games*, only with sleeping bags and a big dead educational skeleton.'

Efe looked even more worried.

'Stick with me, you'll be safe.' Sam's brow crinkled. 'Well, till the very end, when I'll have to kill you so I win.'

After snacks, and a talk by a woman from the museum about why it was important not to touch any of the exhibits or leave orange peel on them, or crisp packets, or anything else that wasn't there when they'd arrived, Mrs Shah (who was just wearing clothes, as usual) called out the names of the people who'd be sleeping in the whale room.

Miss Eagle led them out.

Then the remaining Year Sevens all lined up their sleeping bags and pillows a few metres away from the huge dinosaur skeleton. Billie was next to Efe on one side, and Ruby on the other.

'Now, it says here that I'm meant to play "Get to Know You" games till lights out,' said Mr Miller in his droning voice. 'But we can all agree that would be catastrophically awful. Talk amongst yourselves.'

Lianne turned on her phone and played one Nicki Minaj song over and over.

Alfie and Halid played football, and got shouted at and threatened with being sent home.

They all went to the bathrooms to change and brush teeth, in groups of six.

Then they all lay down and whispered as the lights grew dimmer and dimmer, till the only ones left were from the shadowy pillars and the glowing dinosaur.

'I don't like it,' whispered Efe.

Billie wasn't completely sure she liked it either – there were weird rattly pipe noises and she couldn't help thinking about Raffy's zombie ghosts – but she was still Team Bright, so she concentrated on making Efe not be scared.

Apparently that was enough to make her fall asleep – because the next thing she knew, Ruby was shaking her arm and waving the brightly lit screen of her phone under her nose.

11.47 p.m.

'Mr Miller's asleep,' Ruby whispered loudly. 'Put on your black jumper and follow me. It's time for the secret mysterious surprise.'

CHAPTER
22

Ruby led the way, tiptoeing past a snoring Edmond Hudson, using her phone as a torch. She moved swiftly to the huge staircase, pausing as it forked off left and right, and taking the right loop.

It led them up into a shadowy gallery with a cold stone floor and no lights at all. Billie felt Efe's hand clamp tightly onto her arm as they left the glow of the main hall behind and ducked into a side room, pulling the door closed behind them.

It was lined with glass cabinets, their half-seen contents even eerier in the bouncing beam of the torchlight as they walked further inside: flashes of glassy eyes and hairy backs.

'Where are we?' hissed Sam.

'Mammals,' said a voice behind them.

Efe squeaked as a face lit up in the dark, under another torch.

'Hiya,' said the face. 'I followed you. Can you believe everyone's gone to sleep?'

It was Big Mohammad.

Ruby looked furious. 'This was by invitation only! Everyone else is wearing appropriately secretive clothing, and has brought Required Offerings!'

'Oh,' said Big Mohammad. 'If you want, I could just go downstairs and wake up Mr Miller—'

'Fine! Just . . . don't be annoying. And learn how to whisper!'

They gathered in the centre of the room, surrounded by glass cases filled with stuffed mammals: a wonky-eyed leopard and a tiny antelope called a dik-dik, which Big Mohammad kept giggling about, then stopping, then remembering and giggling again.

'Now,' said Ruby grandly, ignoring him. She laid the large square thing in the blanket on the floor. 'Before we begin, please present your Offerings.'

Efe tipped up her dressing-gown hood and emptied out a selection of Mars bars, KitKats and funsize Milky Ways across the stone floor.

Sam produced six green apples and a packet of

Superfood Breakfast Topper ('Start your day the nutritious way!'). 'My mums are healthy snackers. There's vitamins in there. Shut up.'

Billie added her maple pecan pastries and her box of matches.

Big Mohammad shrugged. 'I'm bringing my personality, innit.'

Ruby pouted. Then she swept all the Required Offerings to one side, produced a handful of tiny tea-lights and lit them, one by one, with the matches, setting them out in a circle on the floor around them. The flickery light sent an eerie gleam off the stuffed leopard's eyes, as if it was watching.

She pulled away the blanket, to reveal a flat wooden board. It had letters printed on it – the whole alphabet in order; numbers too, and, in each corner, YES and NO.

'Whoa! Is that a Ouija board?' said Big Mohammad.

'A wee-what?' said Sam.

'Ouija,' said Ruby proudly. 'That's how you say it – *Wee-jah*. It's for summoning the spirits of the dead. We're going to have a séance.'

The candles all flickered ominously.

'Do we have to?' whispered Efe.

Billie was thinking the same, though she didn't really want to say it out loud.

'Yes!' said Ruby. 'Unless you want to go all the way back downstairs. By yourself. In the dark. No? Good. Now, here's how it works. Everyone eats one of the Required Offerings. Just one. And we put one on the board to, um, entice the spirits. Then I'll send out a message to the spirit world – because I'm very spiritual and sensitive to darkness and that sort of thing. We all put our fingertips on this glass, and then we wait for contact.'

She produced a small glass tumbler, tipped it upside-down on the board, and pushed it around the letters to demonstrate. 'See? Only no cheating. You have to wait for the spirits of the dead to move the glass, or it's not real.'

Billie took a pastry and chewed it, even though she'd already brushed her teeth and it tasted weirdly minty-fresh.

They gave the spirits one apple and a sprinkling of Breakfast Topper. 'Because dead people need vitamins too,' said Ruby knowledgeably. 'Now, everyone close your eyes and link hands, while I call upon the Veil.'

Efe quivered. Big Mohammad frowned. Billie wished she'd brought an extra jumper as her breath puffed out in the cold before her. But they sat in a dutiful circle, held hands and closed their eyes.

'Spirits, hear us. Hear us, and speak through us,' whispered Ruby in a low voice. 'We offer you this, er, apple and some sort of seeds and stuff, and humbly beg you to grace us with your presence. Is anyone there?'

There was a faint rattling from somewhere.

Billie stared at the glassy-eyed leopard sternly, as if warning it not to spring into life and go *Wooooooo*.

Ruby's nose wrinkled up, sniffing. 'Hello?' she said in a faraway voice. 'Is that— Oh! Is that . . . Remington?' She snuffled through her nose again, then gasped – still with her eyes shut. 'Remington, my poor passed-away rabbit? Are you all right? Wait – everyone, open your eyes!'

She pulled the upturned glass over to the centre of the board. 'All of you, quickly, before she goes away. Just fingertips. Yes, that's right. Now – Remington? Are you all right? Are you in rabbit heaven?'

The glass trembled under their fingertips, as if not quite sure where to go. Then it suddenly sped across the board, to land on YES.

Efe's mouth fell open. Big Mohammad yelped. Even Sam looked intrigued.

Ruby bit her lip. 'And . . . was the vet right? Did you die of old age?'

The glass trembled again – then swooped to NO. 'What, then?'

The glass slowly slid down towards the letters, and laboriously began to spell.

M-I-X-Y

'That doesn't spell anything,' whispered Sam, frowning.

'No, wait . . .' hissed Ruby.

The glass sped up, spelling quicker, with Efe writing down the letters.

M-I-X-Y-M-Y-T-O-S-I-S

'It's a type of rabbit disease,' said Ruby firmly. 'That rabbits die of. Famously.'

Sam peered at Efe's tiny handwriting. 'I don't think that's how you spell it.'

Ruby glared. 'Well, perhaps my rabbit didn't eat a dictionary before she died,' she said crisply. 'Oh, poor Remington! If only we'd known, perhaps we could have saved you. I'm so sorry, my darling rabbit friend.'

T-H-A-T-S-O-K

'Well, thank goodness your dead rabbit forgives you,' said Sam in a flat tone.

'I'm sure it wasn't really your fault,' said Efe, gently patting Ruby's arm.

Ruby's chin gave a stoic wobble. 'Thank you *so* much, Efe. It helps to have *true* friends to support me. It's been so hard, you see. Remington really was a special rabbit. Since the baby came, my mum hasn't had much time for me, but Remington was always there to listen, with her lovely floppy ears and her quivery pink nose . . .'

Sam groaned, and grabbed the Required Offering apple from the middle of the board, crunching a big bite out of it.

Ruby looked murderous. Then she jerked round sharply, startled. 'What was that?' she hissed, peering into the dark.

Big Mohammad switched on his torch and waved it about in the spooky dark corners – but all that did was make them look more spooky.

'I didn't hear anything,' said Sam – but as she did so, the candles guttered, almost flickering out.

Billie stared into the darkness.

There's no such thing as ghosts.

There was a clattering noise: sharp, sudden, echoing – and undeniably in the same room.

Big Mohammad jumped back with a shriek, narrowly missing setting fire to his bat outfit.

'I don't understand,' said Ruby in her normal voice. 'I can't really have – I mean, not that I was lying, but spirits don't really . . .'

She placed her hand back on the glass in the middle of the Ouija board.

The others did too. Trembling, Billie followed suit.

The glass began to move at once, slowly, in circles, saying nothing, until it jerked – sharp left – up – then settled into a smooth glide from letter to letter.

B-I-L-L-I-E

Billie felt a choking feeling in her throat.

I-T-S

She wanted to pull her hand away, but it
wouldn't let go.

M-U-M

23

Billie shivered.

It was really happening. Mum. Her mum. Talking to her, right now.

This wasn't the sort of sign I wanted, Mum.

Actually the pigeon was fine, actually.

Mum?

Everyone was staring at her. Efe looked petrified. Big Mohammad was wedging a pecan pastry into his mouth, whole. Sam's face was stiff.

But Ruby looked thrilled, her eyes all sparkly in the candlelight.

'I did it! I really did it! Spirit,' she said, in an excited quavery whisper. 'Billie's here! She's listening! Do – do you have a question for your mum, Billie?'

The candles flickered again.

Billie stared around the dark room, sensing all those glassy eyes in cabinets on her, and felt sick to her stomach. She shook her head. 'I don't like this,' she whispered. 'Make it stop.'

Under Ruby's hand, the glass jerked, and skidded wildly across the board.

'What are you doing?' yelled Efe.

'I'm not doing it!' Ruby protested as the glass slid off again. 'I think she wants to say something.'

There was a bang, far off, but terribly loud, echoing through the old museum.

The glass veered at once to the corner symbol.

YES.

'Spirit – what do you want to say?' whispered Ruby.

The glass spun across the letters.

B-I-L-L-I-E

'Stop it,' said Sam, pulling her hand away.

N-O-T-P-R-O-U-D

Outside, there was another bang, and a shuffling, whispering sound.

'Why not, Spirit?'

Y-O-U-D-O-N-T

'Ruby, stop it!' said Sam sharply.

'E-V-E-N-K-N-O-W-M-E'

Efe clapped her hand over her mouth.

Big Mohammad gasped.

Billie thought she might actually be sick, right there, in Mammals.

There it was, spelled out.

Her mum, reaching across death to talk to her. And . . . not being proud, after all. Knowing Billie's very worst secret.

'Oh dear,' said Ruby, not quite managing to keep a hint of triumph out of her voice.

'*Ruby,*' growled Sam.

'Let me say something back,' whispered Billie, her trembly hands scrabbling at the board, reaching for the glass again.

'Billie, no—' said Sam, gripping her arm. 'Ruby. Tell her! Tell her it's all made up – that it's just you being a vicious little—'

'Mum? *Mum?*' called Billie, pulling her arm away from Sam and pressing the glass hard with both fingers, looking up pleadingly at the ceiling.

There was another colossal bang, then a rush of cold air – and all the candles blew out.

Efe screamed in the darkness.

Then all the lights flicked on, painfully bright, and a security woman in a hi-vis jacket and a little peaked hat marched through the now-open door.

'Hello?' she called. 'If there's anyone in here, I suggest you come out sharpish.'

Sam scrambled to her feet first, and dragged Billie with her. 'Come on!' she hissed urgently, pulling her past the leopard and the dik-dik to crouch behind a stuffed reindeer. Efe tucked in beside them, curled up into a ball with her hands over her head.

But Ruby stayed on her knees, trying to fold the Ouija board and gather up all the Required Offerings, while Big Mohammad ran for the door – straight into Mr Miller.

'Well, well, well,' he said. 'I told Mrs Cooper this was a terrible idea. She doesn't listen to me, does she? No one listens to me . . .'

The security woman was much less calm. 'Candles! Bloody hell, girl! If they hadn't set off a heat detector, you could've set light to the entire collection! This place is hundreds of years old! These things are priceless! There's a stuffed quagga over there, and you can't replace it because they're bloody extinct!'

'Yes! What she said,' said Mr Miller. 'Bad. You're a bad girl.'

It didn't sound very convincing, coming from a man dressed as a pumpkin, but Ruby's head drooped anyway.

'Sorry,' she mumbled, still on her knees. 'Really sorry.'

'Any more of you in here?' The security woman peered around the cases.

Sam winced, pressing her finger to her lips unnecessarily.

Billie waited, agonized, for Ruby to give them away.

'No,' said Ruby firmly, standing up. 'It was just

us two, no one else. And it was all my idea. He just wondered what I was doing, and I made him stay so I wasn't by myself.'

Big Mohammad nodded vigorously. 'What she said. That.'

There was a long, agonizing pause.

Then Mr Miller muttered something under his breath and led them both away.

The security woman's walkie-talkie crackled with static. 'Yep, all clear now. On my way back to write it up.' There was another buzz of static. 'Bloody kids. It's a museum, you know, a place of science, not a playground . . . Last week some brat wrote their name on the blue whale in glitter . . . Glitter! . . . Ban the whole thing, I say . . .'

They waited, crouched behind the reindeer, until they were quite certain she'd gone.

Then Billie sank onto the floor, leaning back against a cool stone pillar. She felt as if she'd been in a washing machine, with all her feelings swooshing around inside her and coming out crumpled and sopping wet. She felt tears prickling behind her eyes.

'Tissue?' offered Sam.

'That's not a tissue, that's your sleeve,' said Efe.

'I'm improvising!'

Billie blew her nose on it gratefully all the same.

'That was horrible,' she murmured.

'It wasn't really your mum, though, was it?' said Efe, chewing her lip. 'Was it?'

Billie felt the washing-machine feeling again. Could it be? She'd wished so hard for Mum to send a message, a real message – she'd wished and wished for it, prayed and prayed . . . but not . . . not like that—

'No!' said Sam confidently. 'Ghosts aren't real. It was just Ruby, making stuff up to be mean.'

Sam was right. It wasn't real. Her real mum would never make her feel so awful.

'Ruby didn't give us away, though,' said Billie quietly.

She could have. She could've pointed at the reindeer and said, *Yes, Mr Miller, there are three other naughty girls over there.* But she hadn't.

It didn't make it OK. Billie didn't think anything could make it OK.

But it was something.

'I'm freezing,' said Sam. 'And this reindeer

makes me want to sneeze. Come on, let's go back to bed.'

They tiptoed out of Mammals, along the hall and down the dark staircase, keeping to the shadows. The main hall was quiet, the huge dinosaur surrounded by strange little humps where the rest of the Year 7s were sleeping. The only sound was Edmond Hudson, still snoring.

Relieved, Billie hurried towards her empty sleeping bag.

Until a torch flashed on, and Miss Eagle stepped out in front of the three of them, still in her pyjamas and bunches, but now terribly serious.

'Oh dear,' she said. 'I so wanted to be wrong. You've really let me down, girls.'

It got worse, much worse.

Miss Eagle made them put on their coats and shoes, and quietly pack all their things. Then they sat waiting in the hallway on one bench, while Ruby and Big Mohammad waited on the other.

Gradually the parents began to arrive.

Dr Skidelsky was first, so angry her face matched the purple streaks in her hair.

Efe's auntie and Mohammad's dad arrived one after the other, grim-faced.

Ruby's stepdad Pete arrived in a tracksuit, with grey bags under his eyes.

Last to come was Dad – with, to Billie's horror, Michael too.

'But – you've got . . . tomorrow . . .' she whispered, running over.

Michael always got nine hours' sleep before a game. The clock on the wall said it was now almost two in the morning.

'Was awake anyway – too excited. And I thought he might go a bit less ballistic if I came too,' he whispered back as Dad went to shake hands with Miss Eagle. 'Though he's pretty mad, so I'm not making any promises.'

All the adults went into an office.

'I wish that dinosaur would come to life and eat me,' said Big Mohammad miserably while they waited. 'At least it'd be quick.'

Ruby said nothing; just sat with her furry muppet hood up so no one could see her face.

Then they all came back, looking even more angry than before.

'I'm sorry, I'm really sorry – I'm actually more sorry than I've ever been, actually,' Billie promised, clinging onto her dad's arm – but he shook her off.

'Save it. I expect this kind of call about Raffy, but not you. It's not Team Bright, is it? Not how we do things. You've let me down, Billie. Let me right down.'

It felt terrible.

She could hear all the others being told similar things, and wanted to put her hands over her ears.

Dr Skidelsky tapped Dad on the arm, and they agreed to share a black cab back to Sorrel Street. Billie sat on one of the flip-down seats, craning round to look at the meter as it ticked and ticked, red numbers going up and up and making her feel more terrible with every pound.

'I'll pay you back,' Billie whispered as Dad and Dr Skidelsky argued in a friendly way over their wallets.

'Yes, you will,' said Dad grimly, steering her upstairs.

She lay awake, listening to him rattle around the kitchenette to a quiet radio, all night long.

Hi Mum,

I'm glad you're not a ghost.

And I'm really sorry I sneaked off and nearly set fire to all the stuffed reindeers, etc., even though it wasn't my idea, and actually it was really upsetting and I am definitely being punished just from feeling terrible. Also Dad is making me clean all the gunk off the ketchup bottle caps and the chewing gum off the bottom of the tables. (He said I was going to scrub the floor with a toothbrush too, but I think he was joking. You know how sometimes it is hard to tell.)

Michael did go to his tryouts, even though he got hardly any sleep, and they said not yet but maybe next year, and I feel like the actual worst sister ever. But he said it wasn't my fault – everyone else there was better and they were fifteen, and bigger than him too, which seems impossible. He said they were all posh, and almost all of them were white as well, and I don't think that's fair. Is that fair, God, eh? Sort it out.

Raffy was so good at being scary he's got a job working as a zombie in a pop-up ghost-train ride on the South Bank. He has to go 'Urgh-argh-urgh' and wear cobwebs and blood, which is fine – except when he comes into the café to eat chips and everyone leaves. I'm a bit over Halloween now, to be honest.

Dad is too. Gloria keeps coming in dressed as a witch and getting green fingerprints on all the sandwiches.

I'm being really, really good, I promise. I will make you proud eventually – it just might take a bit longer than I expected.

Lots of love,
Amen,
Bye

CHAPTER
24

Half-term wasn't much of a holiday.

Billie spent most of it in The Splendide – 'since you can't be trusted, apparently'.

Every now and then the Paget-Skidelskys would come in – without Sam, who was grounded and not allowed out even for dog-walking. Dad and the two doctors would exchange sighs about their 'disappointing children', while the boy Sam slipped Billie notes from down the road under cover of eating cheese baguettes.

> Help! I have been locked up in a cupboard
> in chains!
>   Not really. But I'm not allowed my phone or
> internet or telly all week. I'm going to tunnel
> out using a spoon and escape to Westfield or
> Patagonia or somewhere. Let me know if you
> want to come.

From Bored Sam

Billie wrote back on a serviette:

I do want to come. I am not allowed DVDs at all and the days are very long. Do they have Disney in Patagonia?

From Greasy Billie (I have been cleaning the panini grill – it is actually disgusting)

The boy Sam brought the reply:

They have Disney everywhere, Mum K says. But she also says it's a vile capitalist blight on Western childhood, so I wouldn't listen to her.

From So-Bored-I-Just-Did-2-Extra-Maths-Homework-Chapters-for-Fun Sam

Billie wrote back on another serviette:

Instead of Patagonia, can we go to Wales? I am going to run away to find Uncle Fed and get

*him to do my Hero project. I'm already in the
most trouble ever, so actually it can't get worse.*

Sam wrote back – *I am IN!* – on the back of a
London Paddington–Swansea train timetable.

But it was not meant to be.

While Billie was glumly squirting Lemony Fresh
onto a stubborn coffee stain on the café counter on
Wednesday morning, Raffy shuffled down in his
pyjama bottoms and a hoodie, hair all sideways.

'Classing up the place, Raff – thank you,' said
Dad.

'We're out of milk,' he mumbled. 'I brought the
post down, though.'

Raffy slid a bundle of letters onto the counter
as Gloria rolled her eyes fondly and slid him a pint
from the fridge.

It was mostly sad-looking bills for Dad, apart
from one familiar envelope: Billie's own handwriting, to *Federico Cilenti*.

NOT KNOWN AT THIS ADDRESS, it said
in angry red felt pen, with lots of arrows pointing
to where Billie had written her name and address
on the back.

Billie tucked it quickly into her pocket, before Raffy could see.

'Not being a zombie today?' she asked as he lingered to gaze hopefully at the bacon already sizzling on the grill.

Raffy shook his head with a sigh. 'Nah, they closed the ghost train 'cos it was too scary, and it's all Christmas at the costume shop now. I wouldn't mind if I ever got to be Santa, but I always end up being a tree. That tinsel's well itchy.'

Billie saw Dad's face, watchful, worried. He knew what that meant too. Raffy was about to get fired again, and then Dad would be quietly disappointed with him as well as her, and she'd hear him making cocoa at midnight because he couldn't sleep, and half-term would get even more sad and depressing.

She leaned in very close to Raffy. 'Do you think you might want to try going on that course again, like Gabriel said?' she whispered. 'Just a little try? Because being a husk with your soul sucked out might be better than being an itchy tree, actually.'

'Nah. I'm not going to have time. You remember that band, The Scream? They asked me to join.'

'You're joining a band now?' asked Gloria loudly, slipping a bacon bap into his hands and raising a finger to her lips – *Shhh* – as if Dad wasn't standing right beside her.

'You going to tell them you never learned how to play that guitar, Raff?' he said.

Raffy grinned. 'It's all good, Dad. I can be, like, the maracas guy. All the best bands have one of them.'

He picked up the milk, raised the bacon bap in a sort of thank-you wave, and shuffled off upstairs, yawning.

Billie watched him go with a frown.

'Oof – what's that face for?'

Billie sprayed some Lemony Fresh on the counter, thinking. 'What did Mum want to be when she grew up?'

Dad tilted his head. 'Wonder Woman. Or maybe a wizard.'

'Dad!'

'What? OK. She wanted to be in fashion, somehow, when she first came up to London. Used to buy all those magazines – you know, with a free lippy on the cover.'

Billie sighed. 'Was she sad about not getting to be that?'

Dad prodded her shoulder with a pointy finger. 'She *did* get to be that! She was a hairdresser, you dope. Mostly in people's front rooms, not on some fancy catwalk. But it still counts.'

He leaned over the counter, taking the Lemony Fresh out of her hands and holding them instead.

'Don't go stressing about Raffy, angel. Sometimes planning it all out is a waste of time. Big man upstairs, he's the only one who knows where we're headed. We all wind up where we're meant to be – that's what matters.'

'But . . . you wanted a restaurant.'

Trini callaloo, and brown stew chicken, and dhal puri roti off the big hotplate.

'I wanted to cook! To share food with people! And I do. Lucky me. Besides, there's more to life than work. When you have a family, that's who you are. Being a dad – that's what comes first.'

Billie sucked on her lip. 'I don't think Raffy should be a dad yet.'

Dad laughed. 'Nope. He's got a little growing up of his own to do first.'

Billie wished Raffy would hurry up and get to eighteen so he could transform into someone old and sensible who knew what they were doing.

She wished she would too. Then she could stop wondering – about kissing and whether she'd like it, and if being a paramedic would be better than being a doctor, and who to invite to the wedding. She would have made all the hard decisions, and just get to *be*.

But in the meantime she finished her jobs, then went upstairs to add two new pages to her Hero project: a drawing of Mum in a Wonder Woman costume, and a picture of Hermione from *Harry Potter* in a nice woolly jumper, under the heading 'Hopes & Dreams'.

Hi Mum,

I have decided there should be a thing called MUMIPEDIA, which is like Wikipedia only just for mums, about things mums do. Yours would say: *History will always remember the many pooey nappies she changed*, and *She was known for her impressive Viennetta consumption, and smelling nice*, and *In her later years, Cariad Bright became popular in North London for 'doing the voices' when reading Fantastic Mr Fox at bedtime.*

It is quite hard to put those things in a project instead of gold medals, etc., though. And actually Dad did quite a lot of the bedtime stories. So if it turned out you were secretly Wonder Woman or a wizard after all, that would be fine too.

I wish I knew where Uncle Fed was. I bet he'd know your secret. But I tried calling all the Cilentis listed on the internet till my phone credit ran out, and I still haven't found him. (I ended up phoning Italy by mistake, so my phone credit actually did not last very long.)

I really really really want to find the key and unlock that box. It would have to be quite a short magic wand to fit in there, but maybe you snapped it, and it will be my job to mend it. Or maybe there is some Wonder Womany something with super-powers. (I don't know very much about her apart from how she wears blue pants.) Those would both be brilliant. But a bar of gold or a massive diamond would be fine too. Just saying.

Lots of love,
Amen,
Bye

CHAPTER
25

On Monday morning, on the bus, Michael pulled Billie's tie into a tiny tight knot.

'Trust me,' he said.

At school, all the Year 10s had their ties in tiny knots, as if a bat-signal had gone out.

Big School, Billie thought, was actually so totally strange.

'Welcome back, Seven E,' said Mr Miller unconvincingly. 'Just in case you were wondering, we are now, as a school, barred from ever taking a group to, quote-unquote, sleep under a bloody dinosaur for no apparent reason. What a pity.'

He waved vaguely at Billie, Sam, Efe and Big Mohammad; Ruby's chair was suspiciously empty.

'You five – er, four – are to report to Mrs Cooper at first break to be yelled at,' he added, before putting his head down on the desk and making Nishat take the register for him.

'Will we get detention?' asked Efe as they lined up at break.

'At least,' said Big Mohammad gloomily. 'Though it can't be worse than the week I just had. My dad made me go to work with him. He's a dentist. I'm going to smell like that pink mouth-wash for ever.'

Billie knew what he meant; she had a chewing-gummy slick on her hands that just wouldn't go.

Meanwhile Efe had apparently had to do a lot of praying and cooking.

There was a high-pitched wailing noise from behind Mrs Cooper's closed door.

Sam pulled a face. 'We're going to be tortured. Thumbscrews, probably. Or the rack.'

But it turned out to be a baby: Topaz, Ruby's little sister, snotty and red-faced in Ruby's mum's arms. Ruby was inside too, wrapped up in the fluffy blue muppet jacket.

Mrs Cooper closed the door on them, and led Billie and the others to a different office, for a telling-off they'd all heard already, several times. She gave them each a special behaviour report that Billie recognized; Raffy's was always pinned to the fridge when she was small, with too many crosses and not enough ticks.

Then she sent them all back to class – except for Billie.

'Follow me, Billie dear,' she said gently, as if they were suddenly friends and not two people who had never spoken to each other before. 'Ruby and her mum are here, and I thought you might be able to help us clear a few things up.'

They went back to her office and sat down.

'Now, obviously Ruby's in a lot of trouble for what happened at the museum. But her mum's very worried about her, and I brought you in, Billie, because I wanted her to know that Ruby does have friends, good friends, who have been welcoming her through this difficult settling-in time, hmm?'

Ruby put up her furry hood and looked at the floor.

'Um. OK,' said Billie warily.

'It's nice to meet you, Billie,' said Ruby's mum. She had a round face with a pointy chin like Ruby's, and big sleepy-looking crinkles under her eyes. 'Ruby doesn't make friends all that easily.

She had a bit of trouble at her old school – I'm sure she told you. That's why we moved really: fresh start, a chance to begin again somewhere new without any . . . preconceptions.'

'Oh,' said Billie, because she didn't know any of that. It didn't sound confident-personalityish at all.

Ruby pulled her hair down over her face.

'And obviously, with the new baby, she's had to help out a lot at home, and we're not always available to drop her off to see her friends when they meet up at weekends . . .'

Billie felt a churny guilty feeling in her insides.

'Only she's been quite anxious about coming back after the break, and this morning she just refused to get out of the car.'

The Ruby-shape under the furry hood shrugged.

'We had a bit of trouble near the start of term too, didn't we, Ruby?' says Mrs Cooper gently. 'Missed a few days of school, and went and hid yourself somewhere?'

'But that was because of Remington,' said Billie. 'Her rabbit died, miss. You can't make people come to school if their rabbit dies.'

'Oh, Ruby,' said her mum, in the tiredest voice in the world. 'Not again.'

It turned out that Remington hadn't died at all, because there wasn't a Remington; not a real one, anyway – just a stuffed toy that belonged to the baby.

The Ruby-shape under the hood sniffled, and one arm snaked out to take a tissue from Mrs Cooper.

'It's not my fault,' she said eventually, in a small voice. 'I just wanted people to be nice to me and do what I told them. That's what friends are supposed to do. Only Billie got in my way because she kept making people be nice to her and do what she told them instead. Everyone's nice to Billie. Everyone likes her. And I couldn't pretend my mum was dead because she comes to PTA meetings.'

Ruby's mum looked slightly terrified. Then the baby started crying, and Ruby's mum took her outside to be shushed.

Ruby pulled the furry hood back. The inside of her pink glasses was all filled up with tears and her face was blotchy. Her tie was in a quite gigantic knot. 'Sorry,' she sniffed.

She didn't look like a velociraptor. She looked lonely, and lost, and like she needed a friend.

And just like that, Billie forgave her, all in a rush.

'Is it really awful, having a baby sister?' asked Efe at lunch time, at the picnic tables.

Ruby sighed. 'Very. Everything was covered in sick at the beginning. And now everything's covered in carrot purée. Mum's always busy and tired and shouty. And the baby is super boring. I thought it would be like having a really clever kitten that gave you hugs and talked, but she just lies there screaming, and if you get too close, she pulls your hair.'

'My brother's still like that,' said Sam. 'Well, he is if you break one of his pencils.'

There was an awkward silence.

'Sorry I got you all into trouble,' said Ruby quietly, poking one of the fake knots in the fake wood table. 'Can we be friends, still?'

'You have to not tell lies, or make up ghosts,' said Billie.

'I promise,' said Ruby.

'I still can't believe you made up a rabbit,' said Sam, incredulous. 'And then killed it.'

'It's because I'm very imaginative and have a unique brain – everyone at my old school thought so,' said Ruby. Then she coughed. 'Um. I mean . . . I thought a dead Remington would make you like me,' she explained. 'You all like Billie, and her mum's dead.'

'That isn't *why* we like her,' said Efe.

Billie hoped not.

'You have to not do things without me, though,' said Ruby, in a quiet voice.

'We didn't mean to,' said Billie.

But she had, a bit. Actually quite a big bit. She'd wanted to be the top friend, like when it was Billie and Yasmeen and Mia. And she would always want to, and so would Ruby. But maybe that meant they would be quite good at being friends, in the end, actually.

'Ruby, would you like to come shopping with me one weekend?' said Billie. 'I still need a brides-maid's dress.'

Ruby perked up at once. 'Oh! I know all about dresses. And shopping. We'll go to Oxford Street, and Carnaby Street – and Camden Market, in case you decide you want to be alternative and distinctive, like me. Have you thought about how to do your hair? And shoes? How do you feel about strapless bras?'

Billie opened her lunch box and bit into her double-cheese sandwich. It was the first time she'd felt hungry for a week.

26

The next Saturday Billie, Sam and Efe went to watch the Haringey Rhinos play Hammersmith & Fulham Youth. Billie wore her warmest, thickest socks – three pairs, till her feet would only just squeeze into her trainers – and two jumpers under her coat. Efe made a sign, which was covered in blue glitter and said:

WE LOVE YOU MICHAEL BRIGHT
LUCKY 13

It was still freezing, even with all those layers on, and the Rhinos lost. But it was fun jumping up and down on the touchline. Efe took a million photographs with Auntie Esther's old whirry camera. At half-time Sam produced squares of brown cake for everyone.

'It's got beetroot in, though – sorry. Mum K

put grapes on a pizza the other week too. It's like a sickness.'

But Billie ate hers in three big bites; it was lovely – dark and rich and chocolaty.

A little cluster of Year 10 girls stood near them, all waving and cheering for Michael: Kamila, whose hair was now pale blue instead of candy-floss pink, and Natasha-who-liked-chocolate, and two others she didn't recognize but who squealed every time he touched the ball. They all blew him kisses as he ran off the field at the end, looking sweaty and ever so slightly embarrassed.

Mum Gen took Sam and Efe home to warm up. Ruby arrived, and Billie waited with her while her stepdad, Pete, did post-game massages on people's legs. Then he drove them in his big white car (which did, Billie had to admit, smell a bit like sick and a lot like carrots) to Willesden Junction, where Ruby's mum was waiting with the baby.

'I told you, we can go by ourselves, we are totally old enough,' said Ruby sulkily.

'And I told you, you're not,' said her mum severely. 'And Billie's dad thinks so too, or he wouldn't have let her come either.'

She gave Topaz's round baby cheek a kiss, then handed her over to Pete.

Ruby's mouth dropped open.

Her mum smiled. 'Oh, she's no fun to take shopping. I thought we should have a proper girls' day out, just us three. All right?'

Ruby sucked her bottom lip and looked at Billie hopefully, as if she really, really wanted her to say it was all right. Billie smiled back, nodding. After all, mums were probably good at finding bridesmaid's dresses.

They took the Bakerloo line all the way to Oxford Circus. It was chaos. There were people everywhere, all either walking in different directions to get into or out of or around the station, or standing still and frowning up at the street signs and getting in the way. There were buses and taxis, newspaper sellers, a couple playing the banjo and singing a song about kisses and saving them all up. There were Christmassy shop-window displays everywhere too: snowflakes and sparkling trees.

Ruby's mum took them to Topshop, and Miss Selfridge, and Urban Outfitters.

They walked around the racks, picking things up randomly. It turned out that the sort of warm clothes that were perfect for standing on a rugby touchline shouting were not ideal for a shopping trip, and every time Billie went into a changing room, she took ages to unpeel all her layers and then wiggle into the sparkly things Ruby had picked out, wiggle back out, and then pull all the rest back on, all the time shedding blue glitter from Efe's sign. (She didn't dare take off any layers and carry them out under her arm in case the shop girl thought she was stealing.)

It was sweaty, and hard work, and Billie's feet hurt – but after only four shops they found it: The Dress.

It was perfect: not too girly or too grown up; not too aquarium weddingy or too plain; just the right amount of swish and swirl when she turned around – and it was gold all over; shimmery gold like the scales of a fish, only not disgusting. Best of all, it cost less than one of Alexei's fifty-pound notes. Billie thought Gabriel would like that.

Ruby's mum found a little white cardigan that

would go on top so she wouldn't be cold (though at that moment it was hard to imagine ever being cold), and some pale gold ballet flats. (They tried on a lot of shoes with pointy toes and high heels as well – Ruby's mum too – just for giggles.)

Ruby picked out some pinky lip-gloss. 'Because, of course, a red lip will be too mature,' she said.

'Of course,' Billie agreed.

She bought Ruby a pinky lip-gloss too, to say thank you.

'It's not really my shade,' Ruby said with a sniff, 'but it's the thought that counts.'

They had lunch in Yo Sushi, where the food went round on tiny plates in front of you, and you had to snatch what you wanted before it went past (she couldn't wait to tell Michael about it – he'd cry at the size of the portions).

'My treat,' said Ruby's mum when Billie tried to pay for hers; Dad had pressed a ten-pound note into her hand that morning. But she let Billie buy them all ice creams before they walked back to the station.

'Oh, I've missed being a grown-up,' said Ruby's mum, yawning. She pressed her forehead against

Ruby's. 'Missed you too, sweetheart. That was a real tonic - thank you, girls.'

'Thank you for helping me,' said Billie seriously. 'I'm not very good at shopping for dresses.'

'No, you're not,' said Ruby.

Ruby's mum made a little coughing noise, somewhere between a gasp and a laugh.

But just before Billie got off, Ruby jumped up, squeezed her tight around the middle and whispered, 'Thankyouforbeingmyfriend,' in her ear, before sitting back down again with a squeak.

Billie hopped off at Kensal Green, one stop before Ruby and her mum, and skipped sweatily all the way home as it grew dark.

She jingled the bell above the café door extra loud, and twirled inside to beam at Dad.

'Oh, hello. Have you spent your million quid, Rockefeller?'

She'd had to tell him about the money, in the end. He'd been very cross and very understanding, both at once.

'No! But I have got a dress – *the* dress, the perfect dress . . .'

She began to take it out of the bag, but Dad

covered his eyes. 'No! I want the full fashion show. It's not a bridesmaid's dress till it's got a bridesmaid in it.'

Billie hurried up to the attic, and reverently laid the shimmery gold dress out on her bedspread.

She peeled off all her warm things, had a quick wash and put on clean undies. She carefully oiled her hair, smoothing it down and tying it up with a glittery clip on each side. She washed her hands. Then she stepped into the dress, carefully pulling up the zip so it didn't snag.

She dabbed some of the pinky gloss on her lips. She put on the pale gold shoes.

There was something missing.

Dropping to her knees, she pushed Gabriel's sketchbook and the Memory Box aside, pulled out Mum's suitcase and opened the jewellery box.

She chose a delicate gold chain with a tiny pendant in the shape of a heart. Then she dipped in and picked up the charm bracelet too.

It jangled pleasingly in her hand, heavy and solid. There were six silver charms dangling from it: a horseshoe, a sock, another heart, a snowflake, a teardrop – and a key.

A tiny silver key that didn't match the other charms. Billie pressed the end into her fingertip.

It left a mark: a perfect circle, with one small line below.

CHAPTER
27

Billie's heart jolted in her chest.

Then she felt under her pillow and pulled out the smooth cold metal box.

Bar of gold, she thought, rattling it one last time. *Massive diamond.*

Whatever it was, it was her. Mum. Mum and her big heroic secret. At last.

She placed the box carefully on the carpet and, kneeling down, pressed the key into the tiny round lock. It fitted perfectly.

Click.

The lid lifted easily. And inside—

It was a photo frame. Silver, heavy, coming apart at the corners from all her rattling of the box.

Inside was a photograph of Gabriel. Just him, not the rest of them.

Billie felt pouty. Not that it wasn't a nice photo.

He looked about seventeen, and was smiling shyly, his head turned away a little as if he didn't know anyone was taking a picture. But still, it seemed mean; like Gabriel was best.

Underneath it lay three pieces of paper with handwriting on. Gabriel's handwriting. They were all crinkled and bumpy, and when she picked them up, she could see that they had once been torn up into pieces, then stuck back together with clear sticky tape. There were places where the torn pieces overlapped, or didn't quite match up straight, but you could still read them easily. She smoothed out the first one.

Dear Mum,

I want you to know that I love you, and miss you, all of you, every day. But I'll stop calling and coming to the house if that's what you want.

This is where me and Steven are living for now. I want you to have it if you change your mind. Call me any time.

Your loving son,
Gabriel

There was an address underneath: a flat number on a street in Mile End.

Billie remembered a Steven. He was Gabriel's first boyfriend; the first she knew about, anyway. They used to come to the school gates and take her and Michael out for fizzy lemon from the Queen's Park café. It was years ago, though.

She read the next letter.

Dear Mum,

Dad probably told you already, but I'm not seeing Steven any more. It doesn't change anything - I'm still who I am.

I don't have an address right now, but I meet Dad every Sunday at the café by the church. You could come and say hi. I'd like it if you came to say hi. I don't want to fight. Just coffee, and saying hi. I love you.

Your loving son,
Gabriel

Billie read it three times, but it still didn't make any sense. No one needed to arrange coffee with their mum, they just had it. When they popped round, like Gabriel did now. Not that she really remembered him doing that; it just seemed like a thing that must have happened.

The last letter had messier writing, on wrinkly paper, as if it had been crumpled up and smoothed out again lots of times.

Mum,

Dad told me you're ill, and it's serious. I'm so sorry. Please let me see you. I came today and they wouldn't let me in, but I will keep coming back.

I need to see you before it's too late. I hope you want to see me too, somewhere deep down. Please. You're my mum. I won't stay long. I love you.

Gabriel x

The letter fluttered out of her hand.

Billie sat silent as the sky turned from dusk to total darkness, and the room went dim.

It didn't matter how long she sat there, though. She couldn't make the words mean something different.

Any more than she could work out how she hadn't known, all along.

She remembered Gabriel leaving home; or him being gone, maybe, and coming back to collect a few things.

She remembered arguments, and Mum crying, and the door being closed on her so she didn't see, and Raffy flinging her over his shoulder and marching her up the stairs to her bath, while she squealed and laughed and forgot all about it.

But it was all knotted up with doctors, and serious family meetings she didn't really understand.

And Gabriel wasn't there.

Not for any of it.

She thought he'd just got old and grown up and moved out one day. She thought he always used to come round on Sundays for dinner before he started seeing Alexei – but that wasn't true. She thought he was there the last time they went to the hospice – but that wasn't true either.

Billie felt a cold, clammy feeling slide all around her brain.

She thought perhaps she had known, somehow.

She thought perhaps she'd kept it a secret; a secret from herself.

And now it was unlocked, untucked, and she

couldn't stuff it back into a box or a cupboard or anywhere.

'Billie? Hey, what happened to my fashion show?'

Dad thumped up the stairs, and his face turned from smile to broken heart in one swift drop.

'Oh, *angel.*'

He dropped to his knees, wrapping an arm around her shoulders and resting his chin on her head while she cried, and cried, and cried.

She could feel him breathing.

'This is why Raffy didn't want me to choose Mum for my Hero project, isn't it?' she managed to sniff out. ''Cos . . . she . . . she's . . .'

There was a word for it.

But not *hero.* Not that.

She thought of Gabriel writing those letters and waiting at the hospice, and a fresh wave of crying broke in her.

There was a sound on the stairs, and she looked up. Michael was there, hesitating, looking at Dad. His mouth twitched guiltily.

'You knew?'

Michael could never tell a lie.

He nodded bleakly. 'Not right away. I mean, I kind of didn't really understand it. But then Raffy told me.'

'You all knew. You all knew and you didn't tell me.'

It felt suddenly, bottomlessly worse. As if she'd lost all of them.

'Let me explain, angel – it's not as simple as you think,' Dad said, trying to shush her – but she pulled away, standing up.

'I don't want you. I only want Gabriel. Bring me Gabriel.'

She stood there sniffing, pushing Dad out of the door and closing it, sitting with her back against it so they couldn't come in.

'I'll call him – he'll come, of course he'll come,' said Dad through the door, his voice rattly, and he thumped down the stairs.

'Let me in, Bills, yeah?' said Michael, tapping gently. 'Please?'

But she bashed her head on the door until he went away.

There was a long wait.

'Angel? Gabriel's not answering his phone. I can't

get a reply at their place either. I've left a message on Alexei's mobile. We're trying, sweetheart.'

Billie bashed her head on the door again.

'Angel, please – let me explain what happened. Please.'

She wouldn't let him inside. So Dad stood outside the door and told her a story – about Gabriel, sixteen years old, and Mum coming home to find him kissing a boy called Steven on their old squash-you-together sofa, and how she had been angry, and thrown Steven out; how she had said things – things no one should say – and how after that Gabriel didn't live with them any more.

'She thought it was against God, the way he is. It was just what she'd been taught, at her old church. I heard the same growing up. It's what your granny would've said, if she was still with us. So your mum – she thought she was saving him from something. Or trying to. She was angry . . . There was a lot of yelling . . .'

'From you too, Dad,' said Michael quietly.

'Yeah. It was a shock, you know? I didn't know that about my boy. But I should've been trying to

255

calm it all down. Don't think I did.' Billie could hear his tiredness through the door. 'You woke up, Bills – do you remember? Maybe not – you would've been all of four, and half asleep with it. You came padding out of the bedroom, and you went right up to Gabriel and wrapped him in a big hug. You always gave good hugs.' He sighed again. 'I thought it would change her mind, seeing that. But it didn't. Gabriel just shooed you back to bed, and put on his coat and went. Next day at breakfast you said Gabriel had gone on holiday. To a beach. No idea where that came from. But no one wanted to put you right.'

He tapped the door, his voice getting louder.

'I swear I thought it would only be a few days, and she'd calm down, and then he'd be back home. But it went on. She wouldn't listen. And then she got sick, and . . .'

'I don't care,' said Billie, pressing her fists against her eyeballs until everything went funny colours. 'I just want Gabriel.'

But Gabriel, it turned out, wasn't even in London; was off on some wedding-location hunt, staying in a hotel with Alexei, and couldn't be reached.

Raffy came home late.

She smelled his aftershave; heard him shuffle on the stairs; pictured his face as he tried to work out what to say.

In the end there was a soft knock. 'I know you don't want to talk, but I thought you might want to see this.'

She listened to his footsteps retreating downstairs, and the click of his bedroom door before she opened hers a crack.

There was a box on the top step.

Raphael, on a plain sticky label.

She wanted to push it downstairs without even looking, but she couldn't resist lifting the lid.

Inside it was empty.

No memories.

'I threw them all out,' said Raffy, peeking up from the bottom of the stairs. 'Didn't need 'em.' He frowned, scratching his head. 'Sorry.'

Billie knew he meant it. But he still hadn't told her the truth. She put the lid back, and pushed her door shut.

She pulled off the gold dress – it was spoiled now. Everything was spoiled, for ever. She crawled into bed and tried to sleep. She wanted to cuddle Zanzibar – but Zanzibar was from Mum, so she threw him across the room instead.

She couldn't sleep.

So she waited until all the noises of the flat had gone quiet.

Then she gathered up the pathetic pages of her Hero project and tore them up into strips: the Wonder Woman drawing, and the cover with the silver pen.

She crept down the stairs into the kitchenette, in the dark. The matches were by the cooker. The torn pages went in the sink. And *poof* – up they went in licks of flame and smoke.

Hi Mum,

I hate you

I hate you

I hate you

I hate you

I hate you

I hate you

I hate you

I hate you

I hate you

I hate you

I hate you

I hate you

I hate you

I hate you

I hate you

I hate you

I hate you

I hate you

I hate you

I hate you for ever.

I'm glad you're not here and I'm glad you can't come to the wedding because you wouldn't be invited anyway and I'm never speaking to you again. I'm glad I'm not an angel name because angels don't exist and if they did you wouldn't be one.

Don't watch over me, I don't want you.

I bet that pigeon was just a pigeon anyway.

No love,
No Amen,
Goodbye for ever

CHAPTER
28

Billie didn't go to church on Sunday.

She stayed in bed, under the duvet, putting her fingers in her ears and shouting, 'Go away!' every time anyone tapped at the door.

She only wanted Gabriel.

But Gabriel didn't come all day, and when Dad finally knocked on the door to tell her she had an important visitor, it still wasn't him. It was Alexei, looking oddly waxy, perching awkwardly on the end of her bed.

'Billie? I know you're very sad this moment, so I'm sorry to be asking you a hard question and not just being a friendly person here to help – but I have a problem. Gabriel, he's . . . gone away.'

Billie sat bolt upright, jerking the duvet away. 'What?'

Alexei flapped his large palms at her, horrified. 'No. Not – not like that. But . . . I don't know where he is. We argued. Wedding things, you know?' He rubbed his forehead. 'He left the hotel last night, and he's not back at the flat, and he's not here, or with any friends I know. I can't call him – he does not answer his phone. So now . . . I don't know. I don't know where to look. And I thought of you, because you love him too, and you know him so well. Better than me, I think, huh? So maybe you know where he can go when he is sad.'

Alexei rubbed his face again. He looked exhausted, as if he hadn't slept in days.

Billie held his hand and thought hard.

Gabriel would want to go somewhere quiet, she guessed, to think. Somewhere he wouldn't be watched or asked questions. A familiar safe place that he knew inside and out.

Billie gripped Alexei's hand tighter, then hung off the side of her bed, pushing aside her stupid lying Memory Box and the stupid lying suitcase until she found what she was looking for.

'I think I know,' she said. 'I know where he'll be.'

Twenty minutes later she was up and dressed in a warm hat and scarf, tucked into the front seat of

Alexei's car, her face feeling raw and scraped from all the tears in the cold November air.

'We'll call if we find him,' said Alexei, shaking Dad's hand. 'When . . . *when* we find him.'

Then they sped away, Billie clutching a precious parcel to her chest.

Alexei didn't turn on the radio as usual. He just put his foot down and drove, fast, his gloved fingers tapping on the wheel at every red light, his mouth grim and set.

'My fault,' he kept muttering, then something else, in Ukrainian, long and swishy-sounding, and from the tone of his voice probably sweary.

The drive took half an hour. Then the yellow car swung into Swain's Lane, and Alexei jolted to a halt right outside the entrance.

Highgate Cemetery.

'It's so big,' said Alexei, frowning as he paid the entrance fee for them both.

The paths stretched away to the East and West Cemeteries, littered with crisp fallen leaves. Bare branches stood stark against the white of the sky, above the rows of monuments and crosses, the avenues of graves.

It was stupid, Billie thought; it was *all* stupid – all this remembering people who were gone, when they might turn out to be horrible after all, all these crosses and churchy stones, when God made people be cruel and then took them away and probably didn't even exist anyway. Billie shivered, huddling her chin into her scarf as the wind rattled the branches. She shouldn't be thinking those sorts of thoughts in a graveyard; it was bad luck, or bad religion, or something – and she didn't care, actually – but just in case, it was probably best to be cross with God later, not right now.

She needed to find Gabriel. That was what mattered.

She opened the sketchbook she'd been clutching in the car; the one from under her bed. She turned the pages carefully, past the half-finished sketches of pillars and carvings, till she came to the one she was looking for.

The statue of the angel. Gabriel's favourite.

'This one,' said Billie, feeling a prickling behind her eyes. She sniffed, then took Alexei's hand and began to lead him on.

Alexei was right: it was big – bigger than she'd

expected – and there were a lot of angels dotted amongst the rows of trees and crypts with doors and carved names above their entrances. There were more people around than she'd expected too, taking selfies by a statue of a man with a big beard. But the paths were narrow, and a moment later they turned a corner and it was quiet again.

'There,' whispered Alexei, suddenly stopping.

Gabriel was sitting on a bench in an overgrown corner, just visible through the trees. If Billie leaned to her right, she could just see the angel's wings.

Alexei hesitated. 'You first,' he said, his voice unusually quiet. 'I think you need to talk to him too, huh?'

Billie squeezed his hand gratefully, then followed the path to the bench and sat down beside her big brother.

'Bills! How did you—?'

'Alexei came looking for you. And I guessed where to look.' She showed him the sketchbook.

Gabriel lifted an eyebrow and laughed, just once. 'When did you get so smart?' he said, nudging her. He leaned forward, peering through the trees. 'Where is he, then – playing hide-and-seek?'

'Um,' said Billie. 'He said I could come and talk to you first.'

She didn't really know how to begin.

But Gabriel was rolling his eyes. 'Typical. Run away from the row and hope it goes away without ever having to deal with it – that's my future husband. Do you know where we were last night? Did he tell you? A *castle*. An actual castle with, like, turrets and stuff. In Northumbria. Because why hold a wedding in London, where you and almost everyone you know already lives, when you could drag everyone to the other end of the country – to a *castle*?! Which costs— Ugh, I'm not even going to tell you. You'd puke. And when I told him, no, flat, this is not happening, do you know what he said? *Cheer up, I've got a present for you – we're going to pick it up on the way home.* And do you know what it is? A dog. A *dog*! I don't even like dogs! I like cats! Who doesn't know that I like cats, not dogs? That was it. I just walked out, got a cab, got on a train. Done.' He stopped and sighed. Then he chuckled softly. 'Sorry. Not what you expected when you signed up for bridesmaiding, yeah?'

Gabriel sighed again, then took the sketchbook from her and sat back, turning the pages with a surprised, fond look on his face. He glanced up at the angel itself, moss-covered and worn, the trees framing the scene now grown and twisted in new directions. 'I wasn't bad, was I?'

To her horror, Billie burst into tears.

'Bills! Oh, kiddo, come here. Ignore me – I'm just having a moan.'

He hugged her tight as she sobbed into his coat, clinging on. 'Hey. *Hey*. This isn't about me and Alexei, is it? What's happened? What's wrong?'

'I found out,' Billie stuttered out eventually. 'About Mum. And . . . you.'

She felt Gabriel's whole body go stiff, and then he held her even closer, her head against his chest, rocking her like she was a little girl again.

They stayed like that for a while. Then her face started to feel too hot and itchy next to the wool of his coat, so she wriggled until he let go enough for her to sit up.

'Tell me,' he said gently.

So Billie told him – about the locked box, and the charm bracelet, and the letters – and about talking to Mum, and pigeons, and wanting her to be a hero.

'Only now she isn't even my nice-but-a-bit-boring mum who we all miss. She's just . . . awful. And hateful. And we don't miss her.'

'Well, that's not true.'

'*You* don't. None of you do. And you knew, and left me to miss her all by myself, 'cos you didn't *tell* me!' She punched him on the arm, feebly.

Gabriel nodded. 'True, we didn't. You know why?'

'Because you think I'm a baby.' It came out sulky; a bit more babyish than she wanted.

'No – though we probably thought you were too young to understand, back then, and I think we were right. I was a bit too young to understand it myself.'

'There's nothing to understand! She was just wrong!'

Wrong and awful and ruining everything, for ever.

Gabriel smiled sadly. 'Yeah, I think so too. But . . . Bills, she died. Mum. Our mum. And it was already so sad, and so unfair. You didn't need to know another sad, unfair thing on top.'

'Neither did you.' She sniffed. 'I could've helped.'

'You did. You do.' He put an arm round her shoulder. 'You know what's most sad and unfair, though?'

Billie shook her head.

'She would've changed her mind, Bills. If she'd had a bit more time to think about it, she would've seen that I'm still Gabriel, whoever I love; that I don't need to be helped, or saved, or changed; that I still matter just the way I am. We would've had that talk, one day. I know it. And . . . she never got a chance. To see me happy. Well . . .' He gave a bittersweet laugh as he looked up. Alexei had given up waiting and was walking towards them, nervously smoking a cigarette. '*Mostly* happy.'

Billie glared at Alexei. 'Do you want me to punch him on the nose?' she whispered, clutching Gabriel's sleeve.

Gabriel smiled sadly, and shook his head. 'Yes, a bit – but no, not really.'

She knew what he meant. It was hard to be actually totally cross, watching him shuffling his feet, shoulders hunched in the cold, looking so forlorn as he puffed out stinky smoke across the statues.

Alexei wasn't *bad*. He wasn't a bad person, a bad guy, the villain with the sword and the cunning plan – even if he *had* done sort of bad things and made Gabriel sad. He wasn't a hero, either, making thrilling, noble sacrifices or fighting for the needy.

And then Billie thought that maybe the world wasn't made out of heroes and villains, Simbas and Scars. Maybe we were all a bit of both. *She* was – trying to push Ruby out even though she knew it was mean; deciding to be her friend because it was the kind thing to be. And maybe that was growing up, actually: realizing you had to work out which side you wanted to push to the front, over and over. Choosing well, or making mistakes – but never being finished. Always having to keep trying.

She knew all those Disney films would turn out useful in the end.

There was a crashing noise through the trees, and Alexei whirled round to reveal more figures hurrying down the path towards them: Dad and

Michael, and Raffy stumbling along behind.

'We came on the bus,' called Michael. 'Just in case you needed us.'

Billie wasn't sure which 'you' he meant, but it was nice to see them anyway.

'OK, bruv?' said Raffy.

Gabriel nodded.

'You all right, angel?' asked Dad.

Billie looked up at the mossy angel statue silently watching over them. At the cluster of her weird, too-big, missing-a-piece family, watching over her too.

Team Bright.

All the people who had let her down, keeping Mum's secret.

All the people who'd tried to keep her safe and happy and always all right.

She wasn't, at all, not yet. But she would be. She had time.

CHAPTER
29

They went for a walk around the cemetery – Billie, Dad, Raffy and Michael – to allow Gabriel and Alexei to have a little talk. Dad held Billie's hand.

Then they went across the road to a Starbucks.

'Dad!' said Michael.

'It's not even just a café,' said Raffy, eyes wide. 'It's, like, legit the enemy.'

But Dad ignored them both. 'Today, I don't care about *no cafés*. Billie hasn't eaten a thing since yesterday lunch, and she looks like a scrumpled-up old bit of string, and I reckon a bacon sandwich might sort that.' He hesitated, staring up at the menu on the wall, and the row of snacks in the chiller. 'They do *do* bacon sandwiches, right?'

'Yeah,' said Michael. 'Um. Someone told me. I think.'

They queued up. Billie, who was suddenly

starving, chose a fruity smoothie and a bacon and brie panini.

Dad grumbled – 'They don't even make it fresh, look at this!' – but it was nice: just the right amount of chewy.

Then Gabriel and Alexei arrived, and bought cakes and coffees for everyone. Billie had a piece of ginger cake.

'You boys doing OK?' asked Dad, eyeing them anxiously.

Alexei shuffled in his seat, looking half his usual size.

'Getting there,' said Gabriel softly, which sounded mostly like 'yes'.

'You've got bizarro taste in mopey places, bro,' said Raffy, kicking Gabriel's chair. 'All them dead people . . .'

'I liked it,' said Michael. 'It's sort of . . . comforting. Like, all that time going by, with the statues going crumbly, and all those people still being remembered anyway.'

'*The Circle of Liiiiiife*,' sang Raffy, smirking.

'Something like that, yeah,' said Gabriel, smiling

back. 'It was getting a bit nippy, though. Thanks for coming to find me, guys.'

'All down to smartypants here,' said Dad, nudging Billie.

'Thanks, Bills.' Gabriel pinched a corner of her ginger cake, raising an eyebrow to ask first. 'And . . . I really am sorry. About keeping it all a secret, even if it was to be kind. I'm sorry about all of it. 'Cos it meant I wasn't there, really, not as much as I should've been, when you were little. And . . . well. Mum. I'm sorry about Mum.'

''S not your fault,' Billie mumbled, quickly putting more cake in her mouth so she wouldn't cry again.

'Maybe,' he said, his voice very quiet. 'I always thought – I mean, I always kind of wondered – if it was my fault. When she died. Like I made it happen.'

Billie sat up. 'Me too!'

Dad gave her a look; it had sounded a bit cheerful.

'No – I just meant – *I* did as well. I thought it was because I broke the train set. You remember – the one with the yellow track that ran on batteries and made *chuff-chuff* noises? One day I made the tracks drive up a hill made out of boxes, and the train fell off and the wheels bent and it wouldn't go round the track any more – so I hid it at the bottom of the toy box, and whenever she asked where it was, I always said it was lost. Then, when she got ill, I prayed she'd get better, but I reckon God just went, *Billie, you totally broke that train set and lied about it, so don't come asking me for nothing, you big train-set liar.* So he didn't save her. 'Cos of me.'

'You big train-set liar.' Gabriel's mouth crinkled up into a funny sort of smile. 'Do you still think that?'

Billie shrugged, embarrassed. 'Sometimes.'

'Running club,' said Michael, looking into his coffee cup. 'I was meant to go to this running club after school – she had this idea that I had too much energy – *Too full of beans, you'll wear me out* – all that. So I went a few times. But then my mates at school were, like, *Come and hang out*, and I wanted to hang out, so I didn't go, but I told her I still did, and that was the day she found out she was dying. And then I never missed running club again. Not once. Like I could take it back. But it was too late.'

275

'Raff?' said Gabriel softly.

'How long have you got?' Raffy laughed. 'I got a whole list. But mostly . . . I blamed *her*. *Her* fault. She threw Gabriel out. And then' – he snapped his fingers – 'she took herself away. She deserved it.'

Billie felt a chill in her stomach. She'd thought that too last night, lying in bed, hating her mum – but it sounded awful coming from someone else; an awful feeling she wanted to scrub away as if it had never been felt at all.

'Do you still think that?' she asked, a little bit afraid of the answer.

Raffy shook his head. 'Course not. You can't go on hating and blaming and being angry for ever. And he turned out all right – didn't you?' He threw an abandoned sandwich crust at Gabriel, grinning. 'Bit too good, actually.'

'Yeah, stop making us look bad, Mr Magical,' said Michael. 'Does good deeds for charity . . . helps the helpless . . .'

'Has little birdies and woodland creatures fluttering around him doing all the housework—'

'Stop it!' said Billie, wrapping her arms round

Gabriel protectively. 'Leave him alone – he's perfect how he is!'

'Isn't he just,' said Dad proudly.

'The Angel Gabriel,' said Raffy, rolling his eyes.

She felt Gabriel laughing under her arms, and hugged him even tighter. She understood that now too. Why he was always the special one. The one who'd needed to be told he was beloved.

'You people are a little crazy, huh?' said Alexei, watching with a puzzled look.

'Yup. You sure you want to marry into this?' said Raffy.

There was an awkward pause.

Gabriel looked away, scratching his ear uncomfortably.

Alexei looked vaguely sick.

'Oh bruv, sorry, I didn't mean . . .' said Raffy in a panicky voice.

Billie sat up. 'The wedding . . . You aren't going to . . . ?'

They couldn't cancel it. She was going to be a bridesmaid. And then they were going to live happily ever after, and maybe have twins like the Paget-Skidelskys, and she'd be an auntie, and come round to the shiny chrome flat every week to babysit. It was all planned. In her head.

And yeah, there was the argument, and the castle, and the dog – and the secret £500 – and aquariums and all the rest. But they were definitely completely in love. She might not have kissed anyone yet, but she'd watched all those Disney films, after all, and she was absolutely not letting anyone let their true love wander off.

She turned in her seat. 'Gabriel, do you still love Alexei?'

'Billie,' murmured Dad.

'Shush, Dad, I'm doing a thing. Gabriel? If you ignore all the annoying weddingy stuff, I mean. Do you love him?'

Gabriel sighed. 'Yeah. I suppose.'

Alexei looked even sicker.

'OK. Good. Do you trust me?'

Gabriel's forehead crinkled up. 'Course, Bills.'

'Good. Now go away a minute. Outside. Shoo.'

A bewildered Gabriel allowed himself to be steered out into the cold.

Billie sat back down. 'Now, I've got an idea, and it's really good because I had it and I'm brilliant, but it needs you all to be in it because I can't do it by myself. Listen.'

She talked.

Dad laughed out loud.

Michael sat quietly and nodded a lot.

Raffy's eyes widened.

And at the end of it, Alexei picked her up and twirled her round, right there in Starbucks, while Gabriel peered in through the misted-up window, baffled.

She really was going to be the best bridesmaid in the whole world, ever.

CHAPTER
30

December came: first rainy, then chilly, then bitterly cold, with frost on the grass and slippery ice at the bus stop.

The scaffolding, cones and hazard tape at Kensal Rise Academy were finally all cleared away, ready for the opening ceremony for the finished sports hall. Friday afternoon classes were cancelled. The new name was apparently engraved on a sign concealed behind a swishy blue curtain, waiting for a Secret Local Celebrity to pull the rope and reveal the winner.

'It's going to be Ian Wright, then,' grumbled Ruby as they hurried across the yard, huddled in hats and scarves. 'He's the only local celebrity there is.'

'Who cares who pulls the little string?' said Sam. 'I just want to know whose Hero project's going to win.'

Efe nodded fervently. 'Please not Spider-Man, please not Spider-Man,' she muttered under her breath.

Miss Eagle was lingering at the entrance, shaking hands with the visitors in suits, and reminding all the students to do their ties up smartly. She was dressed in red, with a fluffy white cardigan, striped tights, and earrings with little bells on that jingled when she walked.

'You look like Christmas, miss,' said Big Mohammad.

'I hope so,' she said, beaming. 'I'm feeling very festive!'

Inside the new, brightly lit, shiny-floored sports hall, the Hero projects were all on display. Billie and her friends walked along the rows with a critical eye, giving marks out of ten. There were a lot of Spider-Men – but even more Malalas, Mos and Ian Wrights.

'That's my brother's,' said Sam, pointing at a comic book that was pinned up, all hand-drawn and coloured, featuring the adventures of Captain Samazing versus a villain named Big School, who loomed large and grey, floating on a black cloud.

'It's not bad, actually. But it won't win. It's mostly about squids after page two.'

Sam's Marta project was mostly pictures too, but there was also a long, heartfelt essay. Miss Eagle had written *Excellent work and very moving – well done!* in neat, clear handwriting at the bottom. But Sam didn't think that would win, either.

'You might though, Ruby.'

Ruby's Jessica Ennis-Hill project was obviously the best of them: it now had forty-four bound, laminated pages, none of which had any baby carrot purée on, filled instead with charts, statistics and quotations on heroism printed in lots of different fancy fonts – unlike Olivia T's underneath, which was a poster of bullet points like *Fierce abs!* and *Fast on her feet!*

'I like to think I might,' said Ruby, flicking her hair. 'I did put in a *lot* of work. Without *any* help.'

Efe lowered her head shyly. In the end she'd decided to do her own project – all about Michael. It was huge, a book made of A2 cards with shiny tape round the edges; it stood up by itself and had a photo on the cover cut into the shape of a heart, with *MY HERO* written at the top in blue glitter.

Inside it was mainly photographs of Michael from the rugby match, padded out with recipes of food she thought he might like, and a long section explaining the rules of rugby copied off Wikipedia.

'How weird would it be if he was standing in the Michael Bright Sports & Leisure Complex right now?' said Sam, nodding over to the far corner.

Michael was walking slowly past all the projects, staring up in wonder at the huge space, oblivious to the little crowd of followers that drifted behind him.

'Well, he has got two chances, kind of,' said Ruby, looking at Billie.

Billie's project was on the next display board. It was short; she hadn't had all that long to work on it in the end. But she liked it, all the same.

TEAM BRIGHT, it said on the front. *ALL MY HEROES*.

Inside was a page for each of them.

Dad's page had a border coloured in red-and-white checks like the Splendide tablecloths, with a drawing of his face and a list of all his favourite things to cook.

Gabriel's page was lined with stars, and he'd let

her cut one of the pages out of his sketchbook: his Highgate angel.

Raffy's was a series of photographs of him wearing every costume in the costume shop.

Michael's was a Labrador with his face stuck on, surrounded by kisses.

There was a long essay about each of them: all the things they did for her, and all the ways in which she was proud of them, like a grown-up would be.

Last of all was a page for Mum. There was a new drawing to replace the one she'd torn up and burned. Underneath it said:

My mum's name was Cariad, and she came from Wales. She died when I was only five, so I never really got to know everything about her. Sometimes she made bad decisions, but probably most people do, actually. She definitely wasn't a hero, but she was a mum, and that is a very important thing to be. I hope I will be one when I am actually completely old, but not yet.

It wasn't going to win, Billie knew. But it didn't need to. There were more important things.

'Ladies and gentlemen, students and guests, if I could please have your attention!' said the head teacher, Mrs Cooper, clapping her hands.

The noisy crowd gathered inside stopped talking, and all turned to the front of the hall, where Lianne and Alfie were helping Miss Eagle and Mr Miller wheel the plaque and its blue swishy curtain into position, where everyone could see.

'What a palaver,' muttered Mr Miller.

'Excellent!' said Mrs Cooper brightly, ignoring him. 'Thank you, helpers. Now, I know we're all eager to find out the name of the sports hall, so without further ado, let me welcome a very special guest to begin the proceedings. We're incredibly lucky to have such a superstar living right here in Kensal Rise . . .'

'It is so totally Ian Wright,' muttered Ruby.

'So please give a lovely welcoming round of applause to the wonderful author of so many brilliant books: it's Marina Cove!'

A pretty woman with long curling blonde hair,

blue eyes, and a shimmery silver skirt over pixie boots stepped out.

'Who?' said Efe.

'Oh pfffrt. That's my next-door neighbour,' said Sam, screwing up her nose.

'Is she famous?' whispered Billie.

Sam shrugged. 'A bit. She does write books. Stupid mermaidy ones, nothing good. But mostly she's just Clover and Pea and Tink's mum.'

They all clapped politely anyway.

Marina Cove gave a little speech about how she felt rather embarrassed to be called a celebrity – 'Too right,' sighed Alfie – and especially today, here, opening this new building when she wasn't at all a sporty sort of person herself; more of a sitting-in-a-chair-eating-biscuits type.

'But perhaps if I'd had an amazing hall – and a gym, and a running track, and all the rest – like this, I might have grown up quite differently,' she said, smiling. 'And I hear it will also be used by theatre groups, and for musical performances – one of my daughters will be happy to hear that – and lots more besides. And the wonderful thing is, it's right here, in your school, so you're the people who'll get to enjoy it most. Now, I've had a good look at these remarkable Hero projects, which – well, gosh, you *have* worked hard. So many lovely personal stories. I'm very glad I'm not the person who had to choose the winner. But . . .'

She stepped towards the curtain, but Mrs Cooper coughed politely and stepped in front of her.

'Thank you very much, Marina Cove!' she said, clapping hard and steering the rather bewildered-looking author off to the side.

'Um – what's going on?' hissed Efe.

Billie had no idea.

It looked like Miss Eagle didn't either. She was talking to Mrs Cooper, her earrings jingling frantically as she waved her arms about.

After a long pause Miss Eagle retreated to stand next to Marina Cove, her face bright pink.

'And now,' said Mrs Cooper, 'please welcome our second surprise special guest speaker . . . It's . . .'

'It is *totally* going to be Ian Wright now,' said Sam wearily.

But instead, out stepped a white man in a suit, who Billie realized was oddly familiar.

'Isn't that . . . ?' she murmured.

'My stepdad,' said Ruby, staring back, her mouth falling open in dismay.

He beamed at everyone and made a short, quite boring speech about protein, and why proper hydration was very important.

'And that's why I'm here today – to keep spreading the message that you can be anything you want to be. I'm passionate about your future. I believe in showing that commitment. That's why I'm so proud to announce that the name of your new sports complex is . . .'

Miss Eagle gave Marina Cove a quick shove forward as he reached for the little dangling rope beside the swishy blue curtains covering the plaque. Rather awkwardly, they pulled it together, and the curtain swooshed open.

NutriGenix SPORTS & LEISURE COMPLEX

The sign even had a little logo next to it, showing a bottle of sports drink.

'What?' shouted Big Mohammad.

'Oh dear,' said Marina Cove.

'Bloody typical,' said Mr Miller, with his hands in his pockets.

They all trooped back out into the cold, and watched as a cherrypicker began to lift a huge NutriGenix sign high in the air, complete with the logo on all the sports drink bottles, to fix it to the wall of the sports complex.

'Poor Miss Eagle,' said Efe.

'Poor me!' said Ruby. 'I spent hours on that project. And all my pocket money on photo-copying. And I burned my hand on the laminator. I don't even like Jessica Ennis-Hill all that much. My own stepdad!'

'Could be worse,' said Sam, slinging one arm over Ruby's shoulders . 'Madison's Kylo Ren project has turned out pretty good. We could have ended up doing PE with the Dark Side.'

CHAPTER
31

The next morning Billie woke up with a smile already on her face.

There was music floating up from the kitchenette downstairs, and a low snoring sound – a real one – buzzing across the room from the spare bed.

She picked up Zanzibar and threw him, hard.

'Hey!'

Gabriel shot upright – and promptly bashed his head on the low, sloping ceiling.

'Oops. Sorry.'

He rubbed his head ruefully. 'You'd think I'd remember that was there.' He squinted out of the window at the still-dark early morning. 'What you waking me up for?'

'Breakfast in b-e-ed!' yelled Raffy, kicking the door open.

'Ta-daaaa!' yelled Michael, handing Billie a bacon bap with lots of sauce.

The whole room filled with the lovely warm smell.

'No Dad?'

Raffy and Michael grinned at Billie. 'He's, ah, busy.'

Gabriel moaned. 'He's not opening up the café? *Today?*'

'Not *exactly*,' said Michael.

'Just stay out of the way till eleven, when the cars come,' said Raffy. 'Oh, wait – did I say *cars?* There might be cars. Maybe not. Couldn't say, bruv.'

They both whizzed back downstairs.

'Are you seriously not going to tell me what's happening?' Gabriel said, hanging out of his bed and looking at Billie pleadingly. 'Please? Pretty please for your favourite brother?'

'Nope. It's a secret.'

'Thought you didn't like secrets.'

Billie licked a finger. 'Eh. I got over it. Some secrets are actually totally worth keeping.'

The rest of the morning was spent in cheerful chaos, getting everyone into the formal clothes Alexei had rented, and had delivered that morning.

Zahra from the salon next door gave them all an extra buzz or a shave, and coaxed Billie's hair into bouncy spirals, woven with golden sparkles.

At eleven there was a sudden honking of car horns outside.

'Bills,' said Gabriel, perched on the green sofa, fussing with the white flower in his lapel. 'I know Alexei's going to love all this – you know, traditional, and dramatic, and all that, but—'

She prodded him sharply in the stomach. 'Trust me.'

'Team Bright,' said Michael.

'Team Bridesmaid,' said Raffy, and gave her a wink as he and Michael headed down the stairs.

Billie clapped one hand over one eye, and winked back.

Then Dad appeared wearing a floury pinny and trackie bottoms, and they all yelled at him till he ran off to change in a panic.

Billie led Gabriel to the kitchenette, which looked out onto the street, and pushed the window open.

'Every Ukrainian wedding has to begin with the *brama*, OK? It means "bargaining". Like, the man has to prove he's worthy of his bride.'

'Am I the bride?' murmured Gabriel, looking unconvinced. 'I don't want to be the bride.'

Billie leaned out of the window and grinned. Down below was a white car – just an ordinary minicab, really, but with golden ribbon tied round its aerial – and beside it stood Alexei, looking very fetching in a grey suit, gold tie and top hat.

On either side of him stood Raffy and Michael – Alexei's own best men, or *druzhba*, also in fancy suits. There was a little gathering on the street too – Alexei's parents and cousins, and some people who were just walking past trying to get to the post office.

'My good friend here is a hunter!' called Raffy, reading off a card in his hand. 'And he heard there was a fox in this house.'

'A what?' said Gabriel, looking even less convinced.

'Shh,' said Billie comfortingly. 'It's a thing.'

They shouted back and forth through the window, Billie and Raffy both reading off their cards. Raffy promised that Alexei was very wealthy, and also caring, and had nice muscles. Billie promised that Gabriel was actually very lovely, with nice eyes and a kind heart, and everyone would want to marry him. Down in the street, they all drank mugs of tea Dad brought out – to prove they were good at drinking.

'Babe, this is nuts,' yelled Gabriel, pushing past Billie to lean out of the window. 'Oh!'

A round of applause went up from all the parents and cousins and people on their way to the post office.

Alexei grinned and waved. 'Hello, beautiful fox. I want to marry you. What do I need to promise?'

'Er. Do you promise never to buy me a dog, ever again? Or any sort of animal without asking?'

'I do!'

'Er. Then . . . yes?'

There was another round of applause.

Gabriel climbed back down from the window. 'Is that it? Am I married now?'

Billie smiled. 'Oh no. We've hardly even started. Come on, follow me.'

Downstairs, she had to pin flowers on Raffy and Michael, and they had to give her presents. Then they all got into cars and drove south, far across the city, to Greenwich Register Office, a white stone building with pillars, flowers on plinths, and a large sign in the doorway that said: BRIGHT-CHERMYLOV WEDDING — REIGATE SUITE.

Inside it looked just like a photograph from Billie's wedding-planner book: chairs swagged with golden cloth, and flowers, white and green, everywhere.

Gabriel wavered outside, chewing his lip.

'Trust me,' said Billie again.

So he went in, after Billie had walked very slowly up the line of carpet clutching her posy of white roses and ivy, and held Alexei's hand.

'You have made a solemn and binding contract with each other in the presence of witnesses, friends and family,' said a little woman at the front, when it was all finished, 'and I am happy to pronounce you husband and husband.'

They kissed.

Everyone cried, even Dad.

'Can we throw the confetti now?' yelled Raffy.

'No,' said the little woman.

But they did anyway.

There was more kissing, and more confetti, and photographs.

Then everyone else was sent off in the wedding cars, until just Billie and the happy couple were left behind.

'I can't believe you married me!' said Alexei, looking giddy.

'I can't either,' said Gabriel, looking a bit sick as a taxi pulled up and they all jumped in. 'Where are we going? Babe, where are we going? If it's Norway, tell me now, 'cos I haven't packed, and these socks are really thin. Or' – he peered out of the window – 'is there a hot-air balloon up there? Oh God. Are we going to an aquarium now? It's not that I don't like fish or eels or dolphins or . . . Oh God, are we diving in an aquarium? Because I'm not a confident swimmer, you know that – I get a bit freaked out in water and . . . *Where are we going?*'

The taxi, as instructed, took a slow tour through the sights of London, driving first around Greenwich Park, then along the river, past Big Ben, through the swish streets of Chelsea, weaving and winding as the sky outside began to grow dusky.

'This guy's ripping you off, babe,' murmured Gabriel.

Alexei and Billie exchanged secret smiles.

At last Alexei looked at his watch, then leaned forward and tapped on the perspex hatch.

'That's enough, thank you.'

'I'm on it, bruv,' said a cheery voice.

Gabriel frowned – and frowned again when the taxi headed north. But he stayed silent, waiting, as Billie's hopeful excitement built and built – all the way back to Sorrel Street.

They got out into the freezing dusk.

'Are we picking something up?' asked Gabriel, staring at the wet tarmac of the pavement outside The Splendide.

Alexei smiled as the taxi driver tooted the horn.

The café's windows burst into light – a curtain of twinkling fairy lights in the shape of snowflakes.

A hand-painted banner dropped down behind them.

WE LOVE YOU GABRIEL & ALEXEI

'You coming in or what?' came a yell from inside.

Alexei gave Billie a little push, and she stepped

in first, her mouth falling wide open with happiness at the transformation – but she was shushed and pulled into Dad's arms until the happy couple stepped inside too.

'SURPRISE!'

Gabriel's mouth fell open as well.

The Splendide was packed with happy waving people – family in their fancy weddingy clothes, the rest just in ordinary jeans and shirts – Sam, Efe and Ruby too, waving shyly from the back. There were twinkling lights hung everywhere, smooth white tablecloths with flickering candles and sparkly gold decorations, and balloons hanging from the ceiling. There was a delicious smell wafting through the air: spiced mulled wine, and bread, and hot chicken.

'It is OK?' murmured Alexei. 'You can divorce me already, it's allowed. Only – I wanted drama and tradition. And you wanted quiet and homey. And I think Billie finds us both, no?'

Gabriel nodded, breathless. 'It's . . . it's *splendide*,' he mumbled eventually, his eyes misting up.

At the centre of the room was a cake: white, iced, with two figures at the top.

'You did this?' whispered Gabriel, staring at Dad.

'I'm not just good for a bacon bap, you know,' he said, beaming. 'And Michael did the decorations.'

'Blew up, like, a million balloons,' he shouted.

'I sent the invitations out so everyone knew what to do,' said Billie. 'And Alexei gave me some money to buy my dress, so we spent the rest of that. But – actually, Raffy did most of it.'

Raffy shuffled forward, looking embarrassed. 'I just called in a few favours, bruv. Like, when I worked on the taxis, I got to know a load of drivers? So I got them to do the cars. And Abdelrahman from the warehouse, he knew we wanted to lay on a bit of a spread, so he fixed me up with a few crates of fruit and veg. And then, later tonight, there'll be a band – Alexei said there needed to be a live band, yeah – so The Scream are coming, after the first lot of food. Oh – and . . . Alexei seemed to think this was important too, so I sort of improvised.'

Billie hurried outside to see, pulling Gabriel and Alexei with her – just in time to witness a pair of pantomime horses in costume clip-clopping down the street, pausing to wave a hoof.

'Neigh! Congratulations! Neigh!'

Then they clopped off, to cheers and flashing cameras from all Alexei's relatives.

'Was that all right?' said Raffy, looking anxiously between Alexei and Gabriel. 'I never met anyone who had any real horses – sorry.'

'That was . . . beyond imagination,' said Alexei, looking dazed.

Gabriel didn't say anything at all for a moment. Then he wrapped Raffy up in the closest of hugs.

'Can't believe I ever thought you needed to go on a hospitality and catering course, little brother,' he said, pulling back and ruffling Raffy's hair fondly. 'You're already a wedding planner!'

Raffy shrugged awkwardly.

Dad swept in, wrapping an arm round his drooping shoulders and beaming. 'So he is. Today he is, anyway. Next week, who knows? Always searching, that's our Raffy. Never doing what anyone expects. I'm so proud of you, son.'

Raffy's eyebrows shot up into his hair. He mumbled something that might have been, 'Thanks, Dad,' then disappeared towards the table with all the crisps.

'I'm proud of you too, angel,' said Dad as Billie wrapped her arms around his middle and rested her head on his chest.

She stayed like that for a moment, just breathing it all in.

Then she noticed that Michael was pressed up against the Coke fridge at the back of the café, with Natasha-who-liked-chocolate kissing him so hard he looked like he might bend over backwards.

Billie slipped out of Dad's grasp and wove through the crowds to tap her smartly on the shoulder.

'Whuh?' said Natasha, pulling back crossly.

'No! It's OK, Bills,' said Michael rather breathlessly, his mouth all smeary with berry-coloured lip-gloss. 'I kind of asked her if I could kiss her this time. 'Cos I really wanted to. And – she said yes.'

'Go away,' said Natasha, not unkindly. Then Michael leaned in to kiss her again, his hands firm on her hips.

Billie backed away and bumped into Sam, Ruby and Efe, all standing in a line watching them snog.

'Gosh,' said Ruby. 'That looks . . .'

'Wet,' said Sam.

'I was going to say slurpy,' said Ruby.

'I think it looks amazing,' breathed Efe, her eyes very wide, as she sipped a fizzy drink through a straw.

'You don't mind?' asked Billie.

She shook her head. 'Your brother is very pretty, Billie, but he's a bit old and large for me. Anyway, I like just watching.'

Billie nodded. She knew what Efe meant. She was going to kiss people one day too, probably – but there wasn't really any hurry.

'All right, butt, is this the place?' said a loud voice, in an unmistakable Welsh accent.

'Uncle Fed?' said Gabriel, turning to greet a large, tanned-looking man with greying hair swept into curtains, wearing a bright purple shirt. 'You're here!'

That had probably been the hardest thing of all to arrange – because Uncle Fed had moved to Australia, so it was no wonder a letter sent to Barry Island got sent back. But once Dad had hunted him down and told him there was a wedding, he'd said it was the perfect excuse to pop back for a few weeks.

'Wouldn't miss this for the world, would I?' he said. 'Now – who the bloody hell are you? Who the bloody hell is everybody? And – is it me, or was there a pantomime horse outside?'

Uncle Fed was swept into the café for a series of hugs and handshakes, and Billie was so happy she thought she might not even mind if he twirled her around later, even if he hadn't said hello first.

The food kept coming out of the kitchen, guided by Gloria.

There were speeches, and lots of laughing.

There was more food.

The band arrived and began to tune up in the living room, on the theory that they'd be loud enough to be heard downstairs. (Raffy hurried off to fetch his maracas.)

Billie went outside, into the cool dark air, just to breathe for a moment.

Alexei was out there too, having a secret smoke.

'Is it all OK?' she whispered. 'Was it Ukrainian and traditional enough?'

He grinned. 'I think, *druzhka*, you created a whole new tradition.'

Someone pressed a glass into his hand, tugging him back inside.

'*Za lyoo bof!*' he shouted.

It meant: 'To love.'

Hi Mum,

So, in case you weren't there, the wedding was beautiful and magical, and there were even horses, sort of.

I was the best bridesmaid ever – not being rude – everyone said so.

I don't want to kiss anyone at the moment.

And I don't really need a mum to be proud of me, because I'm proud of myself.

But I think you would be anyway. I hope so.

I don't think I'll be talking to you any more, because I'm getting quite old and busy, and Mr Miller says I have to learn quadratic equations on Monday. This will give you more free time to swing on sunbeams, attend harp school and other angelic activities, so it's better for both of us.

But if I need you, I'll send you a sign.

(Not poo.)

Lots of love,
Amen,
Bye

ACKNOWLEDGEMENTS

My heartfelt gratitude to my stupidly talented and inspiring editors, Ruth Knowles and Carmen McCullough; I feel so lucky to work with you. Many thanks to Lisa Horton for cover art I love so much it made me cry, and to Dom Clements. My thanks, as always, to Annie Eaton, and all at Team PRH.

Thanks to my agent Caroline Walsh and Alice Williams at DHA, for perpetual awesomeness.

Much love to the Sisterhood, the Ts, MG Harris and Sally Nicholls for writerly wisdom, and to my Oxford Roller Derby teamies for knocking me over a lot.

I'd especially like to thank Maria Tumolo, Dzvinka Kachur and Nadja Middleton for taking the time to advise me on cultural traditions and experiences. All errors and inadequacies in the text remain my own responsibility.

If you enjoyed reading about Billie and her family, you'll love Susie's other stories about Pea Llewellyn.

Turn the page for a little taste.

HAPPY READING!

SUSIE DAY

PEA'S BOOK OF BEST FRIENDS

CHAPTER 1

GOODBYE

'There,' said Pea, propping up her creation on the mantelpiece. 'Told you I'd have time to finish it.'

She stepped back and considered her handiwork. It was a blue plaque – the sort they put outside houses where famous writers once lived, to make people say 'Oh!' and fall off the pavement. This one was more of a blue plate, really. The writing was in silver marker that was running out. She'd spelled *Authòr* wrong due to the pressure of the moment – but it would do till there was a real one.

'It's *nice*,' said Clover doubtfully, peering over

the top of Pea's head. 'But why isn't my name on it?'

'Mine isn't either,' said Pea. 'Or Tinkerbell's, though I suppose I could add us. Somewhere.'

'Don't bother with mine,' said Tinkerbell, clicking one end of a pair of handcuffs closed around her tiny wrist. '*I'm* not going anywhere.'

With a click, the other cuff snapped shut around the fat wooden leg of the sofa.

With a gulp, the key disappeared down Wuffly the dog.

It was the day the Llewellyn sisters were to leave the sleepy seaside town of Tenby for their new life in London. So far, it was not going exactly as planned. The electricity had been cut off a day too soon. Tinkerbell's father Clem (who had stayed overnight just to keep an eye on things, as he often did lately) had made a bonfire in the front yard to cook toast over, stuck on the end of a twig, and accidentally set fire to the front door. The removal van had arrived three hours early, and left without warning, taking with it breakfast, their hairbrushes, and all but one of Clover's shoes.

But not, apparently, a pair of handcuffs.

Pea was secretly pleased. Clem had put out the fire before she could dial 999, but now they had an excuse. Perhaps she could locate a kitten for the firefighters to rescue too, while they were in the area. In gratitude, they might offer to take them by fire engine all the way to London, sirens on. That would be the ideal introduction to city life.

City life was something of a mystery to Pea, but she couldn't wait to meet it. She'd made everyone play Monopoly after tea for weeks, for research. London seemed to be mostly about rent and tax, going to jail, and being a top hat. Old Kent Road was brown. According to films, there were also red buses, Victorian pickpockets, and all houses had a view of Big Ben. It was going to be brilliant.

SUSIE DAY

**The Secrets of
Billie Bright**
9780141375335

**The Secrets of
Sam and Sam**
9780141375281

**Pea's Book of
Best Friends**
9780141375328

**Pea's Book of
Big Dreams**
9780141375311

**Pea's Book of
Birthdays**
9780141375298

**Pea's Book of
Holidays**
9780141375304

Warning! These books do not contain mermaids.